'Markham's take on the inside of an ancient vampire's head is as invigoratingly fresh as his story is, by turns, brutal and touching. Stripped of romance, paced like a crime novel, it engages a milieu which most of us, happily, will never need to see – the teen gangs on the cruel, poverty-stricken streets, the 'rats' in the gutters – and makes us give a damn. An extremely smart, talented first novel'

Jack Ketchum, author of *Off Season*

'Markham takes the tiredest concept and re-clothes it in the rags of slumland addiction. You've never read a vampire story like this before... the *Trainspotting* of supernatural prose'

Liam Sharp, author of *God Killers*

'The best vampire story since *Let The Right One In* and a bleak and bloody antidote to the romanticised prettification of the vampire myth popularised by *Twilight*, *The Vampire Diaries* and other toothless, teen-oriented nonsense. Markham takes the vampire mythology and twists it into fascinating new shapes... definitely one for your must-read list'

Neil Martin somethingyousaid.com

'By the end of chapter two my coffee was untouched and cold beside me. This wasn't about vampires at all. It was about the emerging social underclass in the UK. It was about knife crime. It was about the London riots. It was about the social neglect that led to the murders of Baby P, James Bulger and Damilola Taylor. And it stirred me'

Vanessa Austin Locke, *Latest 7*

'An absolutely stonking good read... the Tarantino-esque timeline gripped from start to finish'

Russ Williamson smashwords.com

Lee Markham spent his childhood between school on the south coast of England, and summers in his maternal homeland in south-west Ireland. A passionate storyteller, he has developed narrative architecture and content for some of the biggest brands in the world, including Disney and Playstation, and written for a variety of periodicals in the field. Markham has written and published stories for all ages, and is the founder of the charitable children's publishing house Chestnut Tree Tales in Eastbourne. *The Truants* is his first novel.

THE TRUANTS

RAV

STAY COOL, DUDE.

Rise!!

THE TRUANTS

LEE MARKHAM

Duckworth Overlook

First published in the United Kingdom and the
United States by Duckworth Overlook in 2017

LONDON
30 Calvin Street, London E1 6NW
T: 020 7490 7300
E: info@duckworth-publishers.co.uk
www.ducknet.co.uk
For bulk and special sales please contact sales@duckworth-publishers.co.uk

NEW YORK
141 Wooster Street
New York, NY 10012
www.overlookpress.com
For bulk and special sales please contact sales@overlookny.com

A catalogue record for this book is available from the British Library

Text design and typesetting by Tetragon, London

Printed and bound in Great Britain
by TJ International Ltd

9780715651766

1 3 5 7 9 10 8 6 4 2

This one is for the kids.

CHAPTER ONE

ASHES AND AFTERMATHS

1

The old-one sat on the bench and looked to the east and waited.

Much as she must have done.

The police tape was gone now, most of it. The odd scrap here and there, twig-snagged and fluttering. The mouldering remains of the bouquets lay all around, the ink on the November-rain-stained cards smudged, purposeless and forgotten. Yesterday's news.

He sat there and he watched and he waited. Not long now.

He missed her.

All those years, decades – *centuries* – being the last, with just one another: it does that to you.

And he'd known she was going to go. That this time she'd meant it, and that she'd do it.

But he hadn't *known*.

Hadn't believed it until it was done and she was gone.

And now he was alone.

And how he felt those years now.

Oh, he'd felt them before, of course he had, they both had, but they'd taken on a terrible mass now. Now that he was carrying them on his own. So it was fitting, appropriate, that weight.

He smiled. A sad smile.

But a smile nonetheless.

Not least at the thought of all these mindless rodents, with their tape and their bouquets, desperately pretending to care, or understand. Or matter.

Buried in the guts of the newspaper on the bench beside him was a plea for witnesses to the senseless murder, the torching of the as yet unidentified victim. The article was skewed to the sound of its usual judgemental tune, the song of the terminal descent of rodent kind, of youth out of control, of blah blah blah. The screeching of rats who thought they were ever anything more than vermin. And he smiled.

They can have it. Her words, and he'd agreed, but she'd put her money where her mouth was. They could have it. The rats had taken over the ship. And she'd thrown herself overboard, into the darkness beyond the prow of this world's gloom horizon. Devoured by flame and resignation. She'd gone.

And now he was alone. On the bench where she'd done it. About to do it too.

He looked to the east and waited. Nearly time. The faintest furnace-glow of dawn in the hairline of the trees.

The bench still harboured the charred scars of her departure. He picked at them distractedly with his tough old fingernails. He was hungry. He'd not eaten since she'd gone. Not a drop to drink. Food was cheap these days, but it tasted cheap. He'd lost his appetite and he was tired and old and spent and alone.

He was looking forward to the darkness.

He didn't know why he'd waited so long.

Habits. Old-ones. Die hard.

He almost laughed at that.

Old-ones do indeed die hard. The hardest.

And he was the last now, and so the oldest. And yet this was so easy. The actual doing of it. It was the deciding to do it that had been so hard. The great avoided.

Habit. Sometimes living just becomes a habit, and the longer you do it, the harder it is to kick...

'Gimme what you got.'

A rodent. One of the young ones. The ones that *thought* they had teeth.

The old-one looked up at him, in his hoodie and his low-slung jeans, and his feet playing hot potato with his body-weight, passing it back and forth, as if denial of responsibility was embedded at a molecular genetic level. Which, from where he was sitting, he believed to be the case. As had she. He smiled at the rat in the hoodie that wanted what he'd got. 'I have nothing for you.'

'Don't fuck with me you old cunt. I'll fucking stick you.'

Something glinted in the darkness between them. The rodent might not have teeth. But he carried a standard-issue claw. They all did these days. Slice-and-dice.

And in the east, a blazing in the trees.

Here she came. For him.

He smiled up at this rodent.

'Do what you like, rat, it's all yours anyway.'

The rodent smacked the old-one across the cheek with his empty hand, but before he could retract it it was seized. The old-one had it in his grasp. The rodent pulled and scrabbled and struggled to break free.

The old-one pulled him close.

He sighed old and hungry breath into the rodent's face.

'Understand this, rat: you are nothing. You have always been nothing. And you will always be nothing. You and your rat-children will feed and fuck and fight until this useless rock falls into its dying sun and that will be that. You are bacteria, on a dust-mote, falling into a fire. So take it. *Have* it. Have it all.' He growled.

Sunlight bled over the rim of the trees and ran across the space towards the bench, and the rat, and the old-one.

'Fuck you blud,' mewled the rat.

He swung the knife into the old-one's side.

The old-one arched his back. He clenched his fist and snapped the rat's arm.

The rat's screech ricocheted across the dawn's mist-shrouded parkland.

The old-one pulled the rat in close, eye to eye, and hissed his last: 'Rise.'

The rat looked into his eyes and saw fire in there.

He saw the old-one's face blister and crack and swore he saw smoke.

'Fuck you blud…' he wept.

He pulled his broken arm from the old-one's grip, tugged the knife free and ran.

Behind him, on the bench, in the cold light of dawn, the old-one started to smoulder from the wound in his side. He smiled. Closed his eyes, looked into the sun. And erupted into flame.

'Rissssssssssssssssssse…'

2

Nothing came in threes. That was bullshit. Everything came in a cruel and constant stream that every now and then found a subsonic resonance that drove people, society, to a fever pitch of hysterical wailing and gnashing of teeth.

This might be one of those times. Might not be.

You never can tell.

It was the second burning on the same park bench in a week. And, crouched down once again in front of the same bench she'd crouched down in front of this time last week, poking fruitlessly through the ashen remains with a plastic pen, surgical gloves on her hands, blue elasticated plastic sheathes over her shoes, Anna Hamilton shook her head and sighed.

She'd worked for the police long enough, and seen enough, to not feel anything more than weary. She could see the next few weeks buckling under a fruitless trail of paperwork that illustrated little more than the fact that they didn't know, and would in all likelihood never know, why two people had burnt to death on this bench.

Heads could well roll. Token heads too in all likelihood, probably no more responsible for the general state of things than anyone else, but, well, something would have to be done. But this was, as in the end it usually tended to be, just another thing that happened because this was the way of things. Nothing more. Nothing less. Just another output of the mindless mass that the human species had become.

But then, having said that, there were things here that were... peculiar.

She laughed bitterly at that. That people being burnt alive on a bench *wasn't* peculiar enough in and of itself. The first peculiarity was the fact that it was the second immolation, a week to the day – practically to the *hour* – since the first. In the city attacks happen, frequently ugly, but rarely with the kind of forethought and punctual regularity that seemed to be at play here. The second peculiarity was that, once again, there was nothing left but a pile of ash and bones. No flesh had survived the flames. At all. And that was odd. You'd expect a scorched cadaver, charred on the outside, baked on the inside, but substantially there. But this time, nothing. Ash, and bones. The wood of the bench merely, and hardly even, blistered. Again.

It didn't make sense. It was as if they'd burnt from the inside out. Things like that happened on the X-Files. Maybe.

But they didn't happen in real life. Certainly not *twice*. Week in, week out.

She shook her head again and stood up with a grunt. Her back complained. She turned away from the bench, ducked under the police tape and walked slowly back down to the car. She snapped off the gloves as she walked, stuffed them in the pocket of her coat. At the car she leant on it and pulled the plastic overshoes from her feet and gingerly dropped them in the litter bin on the other side of the path, before heading back to the car and slumping into the passenger seat.

'Anything?'

'No.'

'Told you.'

'Yes, Tom. You did. Well done.'

Tom Hume had worked in the same department as Anna for a few years now. They were colleagues. Not friends. But they got on fine. Did what had to be done. Worked well enough together. They'd never slept with each other. Or ever even flirted. There was no story. No big deal. Tom was married. Happily. One kid, a daughter. Anna wasn't married. No kids. Had nearly married once, but it hadn't worked out and that was about it. Nothing to tell.

'Camera guys have sent a few shots through.'

CCTV. Last week there hadn't been anything. Nothing of any use at least.

She held out a tired hand and Tom passed her a tablet computer. She flicked through the images that had been picked up plus or minus an hour of dawn this morning:

three shots of a couple of men walking arm in arm across the camera's field of vision and towards the south end of the park. Nope – too cosy. Then three shots of a homeless guy, face obscured with scarves and the oversized hood of his enormous coat. No laces in his shoes. He was heading past the bench across the opposite side of the park – it would be the longest of shots that could put this guy in the right place at the right time. She shook her head. Then another three images, this time of a youth, hooded, holding his arm, running.

'Maybe things do come in threes after all,' she mumbled to herself.

'What?'

'Nothing.'

'The kid running?'

Anna nodded.

Tom laughed. 'Yep. Quite the hot lead, huh? Shithead in a hoodie.'

She nodded again and flicked back and forth through the three images of the shithead. Time was right. Direction he was running in was right. But he looked like a mugger, not like someone who had a thing for burning people on benches. Not that she knew what someone like that would look like, but nonetheless. He might have seen something though.

She frowned and rolled her eyes.

Might have seen something.

Such a cliché. But there you go. Life was a cliché.

Then you die.

And bang, there's another one right there.

'Well, he's headed for the St Alban's Road exit. We need the camera guys to find him and follow him. Tell us where he went.'

Tom nodded. 'They're already on it. They've got him as far as the Underground and they're chasing the transport police for their footage.'

'That's gonna take all day,' she sighed.

'At the very least. I need coffee. Are we done here?'

She nodded.

Tom started the car and pulled away. He waved to the duty officer stationed at the entrance to the park. The officer raised his hand. Anna pushed herself back in her seat and closed her eyes. Her head hurt. 'Just drop me home, Tom.'

He didn't look at her. 'You don't want coffee?'

'No. I want to sleep. I've been up all night. If I want coffee, I'll have it when I get in. No offence.'

Tom shrugged. None taken.

They drove through the streets slowly. Mid-morning log-jam. The city had a cholesterol problem. Its arteries were blocked. All day, every day. They didn't speak to each other. They looked out of the windows and tried not to think. It wasn't difficult.

The car pulled up outside Anna's block forty-five minutes later.

'Call me when… *if* something comes up.'

He looked her. She looked at him. He nodded. She closed the door. He drove away.

She let herself into the lobby, pushed the button for the lift and waited for it to head down from above. It descended slowly. Even the buildings had clogged arteries. She sniffed a half-smile at that. On the fourteenth floor she climbed out of the lift, walked past three numbered doors to that of her own apartment. She went in, threw her coat on the chair in the hall, dumped her satchel on the floor beside it. Kicked off her shoes and went into the kitchen. Put the kettle on. Then through to the bathroom. Peed. Washed her hands. Went back into the kitchen.

Made herself a cup of coffee. Black. No sugar.

She cupped it in her hands and looked out of the window, out onto the city. It was a blank, colourless concrete switch-board of faceless windows. There was so much to see that nothing stood out. It looked like a scrapheap. And it went on and on and on. In the distance, glass cathedrals of commerce were hidden somewhere in the fine November mist. She didn't know why she stayed here. She didn't have anywhere better to go. Nothing better to do.

She didn't put any food down for the cat. She didn't have a cat.

She poured what was left of her coffee – half a mug – down the sink and went through to the living room. The curtains were closed. She picked up the cordless phone and hit the dial button. No stutter in the tone. No messages.

The sofa caught her when she flopped onto it. She flicked the TV on and unbuckled her belt. She turned to a news channel and the news was about the news. How the news guys broke the news rules. Apparently some police guys had broken some police rules too. She couldn't think of anyone who hadn't broken the rules and she didn't know why it was

news. If people being burnt on benches wasn't news, then
how was people breaking rules?

But then people burning on benches *wasn't* news. Nothing
was. Nothing to hear that hadn't been heard before. The
news was as grey and repetitive and faceless as the city, and
the people, and the lives they all lived there. Just an endless
stream of events, of no consequence and to no avail. The
news was eating itself. *Life* was eating itself: caught in the jaws
of its own chuntering momentum, the teeth of its entropy.
And the news just a streaming coroner's report on this existential mastication.

White noise. Processed foods.

Fluoridated water.

Greenhouse gases.

Immigration, congestion, contraception, vaccination,
indoctrination.

Indigestion.

Just things followed by things that just happen to follow
each other.

None of it in threes.

That was all.

She flicked across to a music channel and hit mute. Closed
her eyes and pulled her feet in. She fell asleep that way and
she dreamt.

She didn't dream of a time when she didn't feel this way.

Because her dreams didn't make any sense.

Nothing did.

3

Tom had lived here all his life and he actually thought things were getting better. He tended to keep that little nugget of insanity to himself. It wasn't the way to think these days. In fact, as far as Tom was concerned, the only thing that had actually gotten harder to bear was how much more we knew about how bad things were.

And that was the thing. He didn't believe for one minute that the estates hadn't seen the kind of things the papers got all worked up about years ago – he was sure of it, in fact: he could remember the stories in the playground: so-and-so got stabbed. Such-and-such got shot. Beaten. Killed. Whatever. It's just that back then no one gave a fuck, and no one reported it. The knowledge of just how rough things got wasn't as common back then as it was today. Unless it happened to someone white. Somewhere where such things weren't *supposed* to happen. There wasn't that vicarious hunger for the horror that seemed to exist nowadays. The news had been seconded to the advertising space it carried and horror had been commoditised. The city had to compete with beheadings and obliterated wedding parties being streamed live online from war zones and hell-holes around the world.

And so, over the years, the tide had turned, and we'd been forced to look, and forced to care. Or pretend to care. Our suffering obliged to compete on the global stage. And we hadn't liked what we'd seen. And we couldn't accept that it was how we'd always been, and so we'd made quite the song and dance about what it was that we'd *become*, and were continuing to become.

But that narrative didn't float for Tom. Nature was indeed red in tooth and claw, and, given the sheer volume of nature on the loose in the city, it always astounded him that the place wasn't up to its neck in red. Almost made him proud.

Almost.

And, damn it, he *didn't* see our innate natures becoming more red, he just saw more of us. It looked redder simply because there were so many of us. But, looked at individually, we were less red than our fathers, and our grandfathers. He didn't fear global warfare like his grandparents had experienced. He was aware of horrors, god yes, and they touched and haunted him every time, and he saw collective atrocities occur, of course, but the general flow of the tide? It was away from the worldwide industrialised slaughter of the last century, and all the conquest-driven genocides of the centuries beforehand, and towards something that might one day approximate peace. Tolerance, at least.

We were becoming better people. But we still had a way to go.

But this was not something he tended to share – certainly not with Anna, who'd ended up here, working with him in the city, and who had awakened to the full brutal and bloody impetus of our species far too late to accept that it wasn't something that we were evolving *towards*, but something we were at last starting to evolve *beyond*.

His wife knew it was how he thought. And it was why she loved him, mostly. That, and he could be pretty funny from time to time. Irreverent. And because he adored her too. Not in a big showy way, but in a still, soft, voice of calm way. His love for her was emblematic of his ultimate faith in humanity. His perspective. That it was what we were truly capable of. And that in itself demonstrated that we were still moving in a forward motion away from the swamp, and the trees. And to her that made it, and him, and the world, and life itself, solid.

Days like today could rattle him, though. Scenes such as the one he and Anna had attended in the park. Another body burnt on a bench. Tended to knock the wind out of his sails. He was a hopeful man, his hope constructed on the foundation of how far we'd come. But every now and then something would remind him of how far we yet had to go. He'd see and hear plenty, day to day, that would sadden him, anger him, compel him to stand up, step in: violence, robbery, addiction, all of that, but most of it he could find a way to understand. Most of it was fuelled by a desperation of some kind that wasn't entirely the fault of the people he was tasked with finding and bringing to book. It was, this desperation, nearly always handed down, generation to generation, and symptomatic of a lack of imagination, or resolution, to find a better way up and out of the slime. So, so many of those down there did better than to turn on their neighbours in the grip of this desperation, and while he never excused the little viciousnesses and harms they inflicted on each other, or themselves, he did *understand*. Most of the time. It was hardly ever forgivable, but it was pretty much always *understandable*, if one sought to understand.

But what they'd found on the bench: that was one of the other kind. The rare kind. A throwback. A hateful reminder of that germ of destruction in our nature that had probably got us up and moving from primordia in the first place, that had propelled us through the dog-eat-dog phase of our ascent, but which was now as much use to us as our coccyx was for keeping our balance in the trees. It was the lesser part of us, that part that was, that *had to be*, on the losers' page of history, but which every now and then would present itself as a little whisper, an insinuated temptation to give up and to return to the wilderness. It was the animus of the beasts we once were taking dominion over the spirit of the people we had become. And that was an abomination in his eyes. If there was such a thing as evil – and Tom didn't really believe there was, not in any scriptured sense that might abdicate our own responsibility for it – then this was it: the ghost of the animals we once were, haunting us all, and possessing a very few.

He closed his eyes and his daughter squirmed on his lap, sucking on her dummy. She was watching the TV sleepily, just up from her afternoon nap. He hadn't slept since he'd come in that morning. Hadn't been able to. He'd dozed fitfully, here on the recliner, in front of the TV. He'd loaded the dishwasher and made himself coffee. He'd flicked lazily through the Saturday newspaper but had avoided the news. He'd been quiet today. He'd kept himself to himself. His girls had hugged him – his wife knew that he was in that place he went to from time to time, and she didn't ask. She didn't want to know. She knew what he did, and she knew him, and she knew that if he was quiet, and in that place, then she really didn't want to know. She loved him, and she knew it was her job to remain here, in the light, a beacon for him to find his way home by. It wasn't for her to head into the darkness. His daughter didn't *know* anything, but she went easy on him. Clinged a little. Turned up the cute.

And they'd bring him back.

His wife popped her head round the door. 'Baby, do you want another coffee?'

His phone vibrated on the mantelpiece. They both looked at it coldly. The child didn't.

Tom sighed, and nodded. Then he heaved himself upright, pulled his daughter close to him and held her as he stood. He turned and deposited her gently back into the seat.

'Going Daddy?'

'Just got to check my phone, baby.'

He picked it up and opened the message. Read it. Put the phone back on the mantelpiece and padded out into the kitchen. The kettle was rattling its intent. He went to his wife and held her. She held him back. They said nothing. He buried his face in the nape of her neck and let her hold him up.

'I love you baby,' he whispered.

'Love you too.'

The kettle clicked. The embrace was broken. Tom walked across the room to the landline. He picked up the handset and dialled a number from memory. He smiled wearily at his wife as she handed him his coffee. She ran her hand across his tummy as she left the room and went through to their daughter. He took a sip and hissed: hot.

At the other end of the line someone answered.

'It's me,' he said. 'Camera guys have got something.'

He leant back against the wall and looked at the ceiling.

'No, I haven't looked at it yet. Computer's in the car. Just got the text.'

A pause then as Anna powered up her tablet at the other end of the line and checked the image the CCTV team had sent through.

'OK. I'll be over in as long as it takes to get there. Keep an eye out for me.'

He put the phone back in its cradle, went to the sink, poured some coffee down the drain and then topped it up with cold water. Drank it down in two gulps. He grabbed his coat from the bench in the hall where he'd thrown it, pulled it on, bent down and tugged his shoes on. Checked his pockets for his phone. Grabbed his keys. Poked his head round the living room door.

'I gotta go to work. Dunno when I'll be back.'

'Come with you Daddy? Pleeeeease?'

'No baby, not this time. Daddy's not going to the office.'

He tried to smile. Almost succeeded.

He exchanged a look with his wife.

She knew. He knew.

It was love.

There was hope.

It would be OK. In the end.

Then he went back to work.

4

They were the first on the scene of the next burning. This one wasn't like the others though. This fire was normal, and an aside to the main event. And there was nothing normal about that. Nothing.

They'd been trolling the estate showing people print-outs of the Hooded Claw (as the camera guys laughingly referred to him, due to the arm that subsequent images clearly showed was nursing a bad break – they thought they were very funny, the camera guys. Anna thought they were idiots. Tom thought they spent too much time looking at everything through the mediating retina of a TV screen. They'd become detached. Alright for some). And everyone who examined the printout would look up from it and fix them square in the eye, smile and say something like, 'You serious?'

Half of the people they spoke to actually looked like the person in the pictures themselves.

Average height. Average build. Hooded top. Trainers.

It didn't take long before their line of questioning started to lead with, 'We're looking for someone who might have recently injured their arm.' The pictures were on the wall of every hospital in a ten-mile radius, but nothing had come back yet. They'd bring the pictures out if someone offered an 'I dunno, maybe… you got a picture?'

A lot of the people they were speaking to had nothing better to do.

It was shortly after 9 p.m. It was dark, but the estate was very much awake. Those who had jobs to go to, most of them worked shifts. It meant that enough of them had late starts the next day and the place kept going well into the night. It might have felt Continental, except for the bitter cold and the harsh undertow of deprivation that seemed to coat the whole area.

Anna had been uncomfortable about coming to the estate this late, on their own, and identifying themselves as police. Tom had told her it would be fine. Some of his best mates from the football club he'd played at in his teens had come from this estate, or ones pretty much identical elsewhere in the city. Good kiddies. Most of them. A couple of shits, to be sure, but no greater a proportion than came from the 'better' areas. They might have been meaner, but they lacked the obscene sense of entitled superiority that the arseholes with money seemed to think was their birthright. So, swings and roundabouts.

And he'd been right, by and large. People had laughed at them when they'd shown them the printout because it was so generic. But when they told them what they thought the Claw had done, they'd stop laughing. And they'd have another look. And they'd concentrate. Call their friends over and get them to have a look too. They cared. Of course they did.

Who wouldn't?

Which of course didn't change their circumstances, or the likelihood that most of them would spend the rest of their lives right here in the shadows of the towers, fighting with each other for the scant scraps the city had to offer them.

A few of them asked about a little boy who had been stabbed not so far from here earlier that afternoon. The one who had died. Some of them had been angry: 'What are you gonna do about it? You lot just don't give a fuck about us.' That kind of thing. It was understandable. The story was still in its infancy and was mostly word-of-mouth at this stage. Concrete whispers. It had missed the free evening papers. But there were a few vague, 'unconfirmed' mentions online. Tom and Anna trotted out the 'We're doing everything we can…' line, neither of them mentioning that the stabbed kid's body had since somehow gone AWOL.

Unbelievable.

From the hospital too.

That wasn't public knowledge yet.

Thank Christ.

But that wasn't why they were here. Someone else's problem.

They were here for the two burnt people on the bench. They were looking for a broken-armed hoodie that the city CCTV had caught heading into the bowels of this estate. Tom wondered how long it would be before the cameras would actually watch everyone right into their front doors – or even beyond – instead of just safely back into their neighbourhoods. How comforting. But these people wouldn't stand for it. They might be at the bottom of the pile, but there was only so much they'd stand for. Orwell could rest in peace. Big Brother didn't stand a chance. Even on TV its days were numbered. Only so much people could stomach. Tom smiled a little at the facile absurdity of the places to which his mind sometimes transported him to.

Which was when they heard the commotion. Five or six floors up.

People shouting, calling for help. Fire.

They didn't even pause to exchange glances. They made straight for the stairwell and raced up towards the source of the alarm. They barged past an old dear lugging her shopping up the stairs. Almost ran into a young black child in his school uniform heading down the stairs holding the hand of a fair-skinned youngster in a suit. An odd couple that neither Tom nor Anna fully took in and wouldn't recall until later. Too late.

When they reached the door to the flat in question there were people standing outside their own front doors on the gantry that looked down over the concrete square between the buildings. Smoke was billowing out round the edges of the door. Tom didn't hesitate – he threw himself against it, once, twice, three times, and in. He'd arrived after the event at two burnings already in the last week – he wasn't going to let that happen again. One of the neighbours followed Tom and Anna in.

The flat stank. Even over the stench of smoke and burning man-made fibres. It stank of piss and shit and addiction. The smell of bad people. He ran down the hall towards the source of the fire, a child's room, but one that had clearly suffered from surely criminal neglect. The mattress on the floor was stained and threadbare. The boards of the floor uncovered and rough. There was dog crap here and there. And in the middle of the room a small bonfire belched out dark, acrid smoke. An old cardboard box wilting in the yellow and blue flames that devoured it and the melting plastic toys it was clearly failing to contain. It wasn't a big fire. But it was dirty. And it wasn't a person. It wasn't another one of *those* fires. Thank god.

Tom paused in the doorway to the room with the neighbour, while Anna went further into the flat. The neighbour went back out onto the gantry and Tom could hear him barking instructions to one of the rubberneckers outside: 'Nothing serious… but we need a couple of wet blankets… soak them, yeah… and a couple of buckets of water. Quick as you can.'

'Tom.' Anna's voice. Weak. Distressed.

'Hang on.' Something was off about this. It was too… tidy.

'No Tom. You need to see this.'

He frowned impatiently and went back into the flat. He expected to find her in the child's room, but she wasn't there. He moved deeper into the flat, into the sitting room, and saw what she'd seen and he froze.

She was pale and shaken. Leaning against the wall. Her arms crossed, hands pushed tight into her armpits. Rigid with tension.

'Fuck…' he wheezed, leaning back against the door.

Anna pushed past him and left the flat as the first of the neighbours came in with the kit for extinguishing the fire. Tom looked at the neighbour and pointed needlessly at the door to the kid's room. 'In there. Don't come in here. Don't let anyone come in here.'

The neighbour looked at him momentarily, quizzically, then took his word for it and got on with putting out the fire. Tom could see Anna framed by the doorway at the front of the flat, talking into her mobile. She looked back in at Tom and nodded: she was calling it in. She still had her free hand tucked under her other arm.

Tom then reluctantly turned back to the tableau that greeted him. On the coffee table, which was adrift in a scree of strewn drugs paraphernalia, was a dog, dead, bite marks all over his body. Little bite marks. A child's bite marks.

In one armchair, bound, sat a stocky blond male, mid-twenties. There were track marks on his arms. His throat was torn out. Not much by way of blood spilt.

On the sofa, looking as if she'd been laid out, but also bound, was a female, late teens, perhaps early twenties. And once again, throat gone. Her eyes were open and she stared unseeingly up at the smoke-stained ceiling. On her cheek was a little crimson flower. A kiss. A child's kiss.

Lipstick.

Blood.

Tom had attended murder scenes before, but never a slaughter. He knew colleagues who had, and the one common element they all reported was just how much blood there is. Lots and lots of blood. Not so here.

At least, not everywhere: because in the other armchair, here was our guy from the CCTV. Same hoodie. Same broken arm. But for this one, it wasn't his throat that was gone: it was his hands that had been sawn off – roughly, not cleanly. As if it had taken a while to get through the gristle and connecting tissues of his wrists. And his mouth had been smashed too and hung ajar. Tom guessed that his jaw had been dislocated. His blood was all over the place. He could see where it had poured from the stumps where his hands should have been.

Receding now into cold police procedural mode, Tom leant in closer to inspect the damage to the man's face. He could see into his mouth. And what he saw chilled him.

The man's teeth had all been removed. Smashed from his skull. Not a single one left. Tom stood upright and backed up to the wall. His brain did some quick calculations and nothing added up. The fire was hopeless if the firebug had intended it to destroy the scene of the crime. The murders were savage. Two of them bloodless.

But the scene hadn't been abandoned.

It had been *mounted*.

It was as if the scene were only pretending to be hiding evidence, with the fire, and the missing hands and teeth. It was as if the scene had something to say.

But if it did, then he didn't want to know what it was.

It mocked him.

It was the abyss and, as he looked into it, he could feel its dead-eyed glare staring right back at him. Smiling.

He could see its teeth.

And it scared him.

CHAPTER TWO

INFECTION AND AWAKENINGS

1

The banging on the door doesn't wake the child.

The child is already awake.

He lies there, on his mattress, on the floor, in the half-light from the hall, in the filth of his days-old nappy and rolls his eyes towards the door and the cacophony beyond.

The dog has started barking. Snarling and yelping. Not yapping though. It's too big to yap. It's a big black shadow of a dog with a boulder for a head and it is beastly.

The boy's night clothes are damp. The saturated nappy is seeping. The bare mattress stained, and thin, and lumpy.

He lies there and tilts his head and looks disinterestedly at the bedroom door, beyond which the dog is going mental and the front door is being walloped.

'Ste mate, you there? Open up, mate…'

Mutterings from the room further down the hall.

Swearing.

Footsteps. 'Tell 'im to fuck off, yeah?' The boy's mother. 'We got a fuckin' kid innit? Fuck's sake.'

'Who's that?' Steven – 'Ste' – is at the front door now.

'It's me mate, it's Cal. Lemme in, yeah?'

'It's not even fucking eight in the…' The dog is still barking and yelping and out of control. The boy hears Ste hiss, and then the dull thud of his boot piling into the dog's side. The dog squeals, and arfs, and the boy knows how he feels. 'Will you shut the fuck up. Go on, fuck off. Get back in there. Fucking dog. It's fucking eight in the morning Cal, what the fuck do you want?'

'What do you think I fucking want Ste. You want me to make an announcement or what? Open the door man.'

A pause. And then a muttering under breath. And then the door being unlatched and opened.

'You're not letting the twat in are you Ste?' The boy's mother, hollering from the room next door. 'I thought I told you to tell him to…'

'Donnashutup! It's not like…' Ste's holler runs out of steam and dovetails into a whispered, '…Jesus Christ Cal… what happened your arm?'

'Don't ask. You got any?'

'Course I got some. But what happened your arm?'

'I said don't ask, didn't I? Fuck's sake, man, just sort me out…'

The front door closes and a shamble of footsteps hustle back down the hall to the front room. The snicker of the dog's claws on the linoleum. A whistling whine of bruised displeasure.

Then the sound of muffled conversation from the front room.

The hushings of a debrief.

And this is something new. The hush.

This is new to the child. Hush.

The child has existed in a cloud of screech since his nine months on remand in his mother's polluted womb prior to the sentence of life, and this hush is something new. It piques his curiosity. And his curiosity sits him up and gets him out of bed.

His head itches. He can feel things crawling in his hair. He scratches at them, but it makes no difference. He ignores, as he has now become used to doing, the ache of the bruises on his body. Winces silently at the tightness of skin round the scabs on his leg where the dog has bitten him. His nappy hangs down between his knees and stinks. But he's up. And he toddles to the door.

The voices remain hushed as he creeps down the hall. He reaches the door, halfway shut, but open enough for him to peep round and into the room.

Ste has got his spoon, and is holding the lighter under it. It smoulders and steams and quietly crackles. There is a spike on the table in front of him. The child knows that Ste will point the spike into the spoon in a moment and draw muddy water up into the cylinder. How it goes.

Cal is sitting in an armchair, nursing his arm. It's a funny shape, his arm. Wonky. Wrong. His lips are drawn and his teeth hiss and his eyes are wincing.

The child's mother sits in another armchair next to Cal. She smokes a cigarette and looks pissed off and glances from Cal to Ste and then back to the TV.

The TV has on what it always has on. Naked men doing things to a naked girl. The men seem angry. The girl seems… caught. The child doesn't understand it. But it seems sad. He doesn't know why.

The dog is curled up beneath the TV, pretending to mind its own business. Nervously. Eyes flicking left and right.

Ste does the thing with the spike and passes it across to Cal. Cal moves to take the spike, lets go his wonky arm and hisses in agony. 'Ste, man… you're gonna have to help me… my arm's fucked mate…'

Ste looks at him with the barest of concern. Then he gets up and starts round the table. Donna glances, grimaces, returns to the TV, stubs out her cigarette, lights another.

On the floor, just inside the door, the child sees a coat. Cal's coat. And something in its pocket. Metal. The child toddles in. No one notices. Except the dog, who lifts his head and looks at him.

The child reaches down and takes the handle of the knife, pulls it from the coat.

Ste sticks the needle into Cal's arm and plunges.

Cal sighs and waits and sighs again.

Ste pulls the needle free and throws it on the table. 'That's a tenner for that… you better have it.'

'I have, mate… it's in my…'

The child howls.

He's touched the blade and it has seared his finger and

drawn blood. A thin slither slice across the pad. But it *burns*. It burns so much. It's like nothing the child has ever felt. And he's felt plenty.

His mother drops her cigarette and swivels to face him in fright, but without concern. Annoyed.

Cal also jolts in fright, then shouts in pain as his arm complains.

The dog leaps to his feet and barks and slavers at the boy.

And Ste, he stumbles over the coffee table behind his legs, almost goes down. Then he swings a kick at the dog, hits him under the jaw. The dog's teeth snap shut with an audible click, puncturing its tongue. The dog yowls yet again, and then cowers.

Then Ste turns to the howling child, strides across the room and swings a fist into the boy's chest.

'Fuck off back to your room, Petey.'

The child feels something snap and move and burst.

All the air in his body leaves him and refuses to return.

But still the pain in his finger screams loudest.

He stumbles back and drops the knife.

'Back to your room, Peter,' Ste repeats, cold blue eyes wide and livid.

Peter turns and toddles away, stumbling.

Something feels different this time.

He snatches at a breath, but can't seize it.

The pain is moving away from him.

He is moving away from himself.

He drifts back into his room. Back onto his flea-ridden bed.

He lowers himself down onto his back, and feels different.

He tries to steal another breath, but can't find one.

He lifts his wounded finger up before his face and looks at it. So small an injury, compared to the others. But so *loud*. Still. Even from this far away.

He lays his hand back down by his side and doesn't try to take any more breaths.

Then he closes his eyes.

And he dies.

2

It isn't how I'd expected it to be.

Initially, there is nothing, not even a *me* to have expectations.

And *that*, that void, that *absence*: *that* was what I had expected.

No dreams of tunnels leading to light for me. Too old for all that nonsense. No expectation of her waiting for me in some ephemeral form, floating in some other place where nothing could touch us.

No.

What I had expected, and had anticipated, was nothing. An end to all things.

And peace.

It was what I had hoped for as I had sat on the bench and remembered her and waited for the sun to rise and devour me.

And for a time, that is what I got.

But then it started to slip away.

The darkness beyond the end of my life, after the fire and the pain, started to recede the moment the child started screaming. And from the infinite side of the outside of time, that scream echoed for what felt an eternity.

And how I tried to ignore it because I knew what it presaged.

I'd felt this before – this pouring of my self into the self of another. It was what I felt every time I'd ever fed: I'd pour into my prey, and then drink my self back into myself, leaving my prey a pallid husk of what they had once been when their heart had still skittered. The pale opposite of their shadow. Lifeless and bloodless and gone.

It had been some time since I'd left myself in one of them and had allowed them to live. If living is what it is called. Making them like me is a young one's game, and I'd long outgrown it. Leaving splinters of my self, unleashed and entwined with the will of these rats, had diminished me and given them ideas beyond their capacity. That was a time of frenzy. And they too had over-shared, splintered my already splintered self yet further, passing me on and on until I was a ghost haunting the psyche of a mindless horde. A plague.

A virus.

It took me centuries to track them down, one by one, and devour them. Until there was only me left.

And her. Us.

We never spoke of who had been the first – me, or her – but we both felt the same: that it needed to be just us. That we were monoliths, not pestilence. Gods, not men. I wondered how it started, really started, our *otherness*. I wondered if we'd once been prey ourselves to the original, or if one of us had perhaps been the first. But centuries as a horde had clouded the linearity of our memory, our history. We couldn't remember. Memory had blurred. I couldn't be sure if the splinters of self that we'd collected back had started here, with us, or if it was just chance that the will of the super-self, maturing and wanting to be whole again, had concluded with us. Perhaps, on our way back to wholeness, we'd devoured our Adam and our Eve. Perhaps. Perhaps...

It had been a bloody and dangerous time. And we'd all wanted to devour each other. Until there were just the two of us left.

And when at last we became two, we simply wandered and watched, and took what we needed. We dined with kings, and feasted on queens. We went everywhere until there was nowhere left to go, and saw everything until there was nothing left to see, and we sought to find an omega point in the narrative of history. And we found none. Nothing was going anywhere. Everything was going nowhere.

And we wearied. She wearied. And she wore me down.

And it all came to an end on that bench.

Her first.

Then me.

Consigned to the darkness by the light of the sun.

And then the child screams and I feel that pull, that drag, that oh-so-familiar spiral and slump of self into someone else, and confusion reigns. Because I have no hands with which to grab the child, no arms with which to restrain it, no teeth with which to rip it and drain it. I have no means by which I can drink myself back in.

Because I am gone. And this makes no sense.

And then something punches me in the chest and time accelerates and the scream collapses in my chest.

I have no chest, but I feel something snap and move and burst in there.

All the air in my body leaves me and refuses to return.

But a pain in my finger screams louder. Loudest.

I stumble back and drop something.

'Back to your room Peter.' The voice is unfamiliar. It bubbles through a gauze of disconnection and disorientation. I'm not quite here. Almost, but not quite.

I turn and stumble away.

Something feels different this time. The self in here with me has no words, just notions. I wonder if it is an animal. But something feels different to that other self. The violence, that's nothing new. The pain: same. But the sense that something broke this time. That *is* new.

I snatch at a breath, but can't seize it.

I allow him – for it is a 'him', clarity is blooming, as it always does – I allow him to take us back into his room. Back onto his flea-ridden bed.

The boy whispers his name to me, in here, and his name is Peter.

He lowers himself down onto his back, and feels different.

He feels not alone. He feels me.

He tries to steal another breath, but can't find one.

He lifts his wounded finger up before his face and looks at it. So small an injury, compared to the others. But so *loud*. Still.

That is the wound by which I entered him. I know it.

How has this happened?

He lays his hand back down by his side and doesn't try to take any more breaths.

Then he closes his eyes.

And he dies.

For just a moment, he dies, and he submits, and he gives himself to me. This feral little rat-child kneels before me and prays for my grace.

I give it to him.

Then I open our eyes.

And we rise.

3

It is mid-morning before the winter sun swings out and around the tower block and starts to peep through the yellowed net that hangs across the little rat's window.

We have lain here, still, ever since his rib was broken and his respiratory system failed. We have lain here, watching the light manifest in the window, waiting.

The rib has already started to knit. I can feel it mend. Perhaps not quite evenly, but not a major problem. It will probably shift again when we move, and will continue to shift for a day or two. But it *will* stick. He is more me than him now, and I will absorb any adjustments to his physical being as we go. We will take it in our stride. It is how I do things. It is in my nature.

We lie here and watch the window and wait for the light to be a problem.

Perhaps the day will be dull enough, and the danger will pass.

Perhaps the alignment of the building itself will provide enough shade in which we can lurk.

We will see.

We lie here and pick lice from our hair and eat them. Little snacks. We are now the top parasite, devouring the parasites that dare to feed on us.

This amuses me. Somewhat.

After the initial explosion of violence, after the murder of the rat-child, the volume rapidly dropped in the adjoining room. The filth the rats put in their veins dumbing them down, shutting them up. At some point after that the outsider gathered up his things and sloped off back to his own nest.

A short while later the dog whimpers. The man-rat swears at it dismissively. It pads softly into the hall, pushes the rat-child's door open and walks sneakily into the room. It looks across at us from the doorway and growls softly in the back of its throat. We look at it, and it looks back at us, and I hide myself as best I can, deep inside the child.

Animals, particularly dogs, sense my kind. The *old-kind*. And they fear us. And fear sometimes makes them behave stupidly. Aggressively. And I can't afford for that to happen.

Not yet.

So the dog growls at the child, threatens him – *this is between you and me, got it?* – then it walks over to a corner of the room, where a mouldering cardboard box spews toys as damaged by neglect as the child himself, cocks its leg and pisses. The cardboard box takes the brunt of the shower, a small rivulet of amber stench trickling back across the uncarpeted boards of the floor to the bed, where some of it soaks into the child's mattress, while the rest pools along its edge.

The dog leans down and sniffs at its mess, drinks some of it, looks up at us and then turns and leaves the room. It knows to make its mess in here. The rats won't notice it.

I bare our teeth at the door once it has gone.

This situation will not be allowed to prevail.

But my own situation takes priority and I need to understand how I came to be here. Trapped in the body of a rat-child when I should have been gone. Risen.

Dust.

I rifle through the memory of the child, and return to the morning. The vortex-like drag from fire-bestowed peace to here. Hell. Through this wound on our finger.

But how?

I close our eyes and head into him. I wander back into the room of hours before, in the mind of the child, the foul playground of his memory. I creep in with him, and I see the knife, the curiously scorched filigree of its blade. There is something burnt into it and it whispers to us. It is impossible to resist.

We touch it, and we scream.

And all hell breaks loose. But this time I slow the explosion down, and observe the blossoming of the violence in detail. Looking for an answer.

The child's screech annihilates the sordid calm that preceded it and the three junk-rats become swiftly animated. One of them, the mother, drops her cigarette and turns to snarl at us, her son… the father, if that is what he is, this *Ste*… he falls back against the table, nearly goes over and attacks the barking dog.

All of this in the slowest of motions.

And the third of them, he jolts and then howls and hisses through gritted teeth, holding one arm with his other hand, nursing it as if broken.

Then he turns to us. Teeth a-hiss. Furious eyes. Spittle at the corners of his mouth.

And I know him.

I *see* him.

I hear his voice again as he speaks to me on the bench, just before I snapped his arm.

'Fuck you blud…', and I wonder, is he haunting me or am I haunting him? Is that what this is? In my own memory I feel the knife plunge once more into my flank, I feel the sun take hold of me, and the blade, and I feel it forge us together, binding us.

And I know now how this has all come to pass. I don't understand it, but I know.

I lie there on the bed, breathing in the ammonia-fumed fug of dog waste, eating the bugs that graze on me, watching the window, biding my time and plotting my next move.

We need to find the knife. *I* need to find the knife.

I pull us up from the bed and the splintered rib squalls. The child wants to cry, but I forbid it. I can feel the child pulling at the muscles of its face, trying to force them into that caul that always presages infant mewling, and I slap it down. *No, rat. No noise.* And he acquiesces. He understands this form of negotiation. His rat-tail curls yet further between his legs.

We move quietly to the door, and peer round and out into the hall. Sunlight falls through the grimy, frosted window of the front door. Hardly an Elysian sunbeam, but enough at least to trap us in here for the time being.

I take us back to the bed and lie us down. This time will be best spent allowing the rib to knit. If the knife is still here in this nest, it won't go anywhere without me hearing it leave, and if it's already gone, then we will have to think of how to find it and take it back.

But for now, rest.

And so we lie here.

The window threatens to throw the sun our way for a brief spell in the afternoon, but then something shuts it off. Probably another tower. And once it is extinguished, I know it is safe to venture out from the room and look for the knife.

The dog hears us move across the room and comes to meet us at the door. Once again I retreat into the child and allow him to deal with the beast. The boy cowers and backs away. The dog pulls its lips back and bares its teeth, but doesn't make a sound. It glances back over its shoulder. Then it pushes its way into the rat-child's room and allows itself a low, rumbling snarl.

And this is good.

Because this time I am ready.

Once the dog has moved fully into the room I take full control of the child and reveal myself to the dog. The hound's eyes widen and his lips pull back from his teeth in fearful aggression. I leap first. Up and onto the top of his snout. He leaps back in shock, whimpers but doesn't bark. For the moment he is too surprised to mount any form of defence, he just writhes and shakes his blocky head, trying to throw us off.

I clamp our chubby baby legs round his muzzle and tighten them, locking his jaws closed. He crashes back against the wall of the room, head still thrashing left and right, and I can feel a desperate howl starting to brew. I throw our arms round his throat and choke it off.

And then we hold on until he starts to fade. He skitters blindly around the room, and manages to squeeze out a feeble whistle as he thrashes for his life. Eventually he falls to the floor, unconscious, but not yet dead. He's no use to us dead.

I look down on him, his eyes rolled back and slightly open, tongue lolling from the side of his mouth.

Then we get down on our knees and examine his foreleg – there is a vein here that will do. We sniff it out, and then we bite. Our milk teeth aren't built for this kind of work, but they're all we've got and so we make them suffice. We gnaw our way through, we tap in and we take a drink. But not too much. It's cheap and it's nasty, but it will sate us for now.

And when the dog awakens, we won't be alone.

Not any more.

Small steps.

We drop the dog's paw and stand, ready to search the other room for the knife, when it happens again. That pulling away and pouring into. And the I that has possessed this rat-child is suddenly sundered, ripped in two and poured into another rat somewhere else entirely. We, Peter and I, fall to our knees and forward, dizzy, agonised, a Himalayan buzzing tearing through our whole being.

This is difficult. Almost impossible. Then it is done and I am here, and I am there. And the there I find myself transported to is some other corner of this concrete hell, shadow-ridden and unsafe. There is a hole in my leg, and two rat-youths are looking down at me as I lie there on the ground, and they are laughing. And there, in the left hand of one of the rat-youths, is the knife.

It is out there. Unleashed. Spilling me into the scum of all creation.

Laughing as it goes.

The rat-youths skip away into the shadows, laughing and whooping, kicking cans and spitting. Then a street-rat comes to aid this new rat-child I've infected, his face swaddled in filthy rags and lurking within the shadowed confines of an oversized hood: the fell uniform of the so-called meek that the good Lord saw fit to bequeath to the earth. He turns our face to his, this homeless street-rat, and says, 'Look at me, child.'

The rat-child is dazed and adrift in here, and so I look at this filthy vermin.

I look at him. I show myself and I speak to him. And he backs away.

As well he might.

Then this new rat-child drags himself away, oblivious of me within him, oblivious of everything other than his idiot need to get home, back to his nest, where he thinks he will be safe. He drags himself away, and makes it as far as the sanctuary of a fetid stairwell. A pack of work-rats loitering there tie his leg, *our* leg, and hold our hand and tell us everything will be OK, and do nothing for him as he slips into the night.

And back in the room, with the baby and the dog, I understand that things are now even worse than I'd thought.

CHAPTER THREE

TRUANCY AND TERROR

1

They should have been at school but had better things to do. There were things to take and things to break, and there was nothing in any classroom that came close to those imperatives.

They couldn't head back to the flat until John's mum had fucked off out. She didn't care whether they were at school or not. It's just that she was a bitch. So for now they skulked and they lurked, dragging their toes across the floor as they walked, ducking into shops that didn't recognise them and hadn't banned them. Sitting on cold, damp bus-stop benches drinking shoplifted alcopops, and calling people names.

The other kids knew to avoid them, but sometimes John and Bobby would latch on to the more meek and aggravate and pester until they were either told to get lost, or until the pestered had made it too close to school for John and Bobby to go any further. The amount of effort they actually put into avoiding effort was quite something. They were dedicated. Focused. And there was a part of them that desperately wanted to be a part of the world they laughed and spat at. But their stubborn pre-teen minds would never allow that. They would never submit.

They were both twelve years old.

And so they kicked around the clogged school-run streets of the city, keeping their heads down and their necks out. Mixing their signals. Crying for help. Being ignored.

Abandoned.

Alone.

And adrift.

They did this for two hours, as they did most term-time weekdays, then they headed back in the direction of the flat. They hung back and watched John's mum scuttle out and away down towards the bus stop. John didn't know where she went. Or what she did when she got there. Sometimes she came back with money. Sometimes she came back with other stuff. They headed up and around and in, each casually discarding their drained bottles in the stairwell on the way up.

They let themselves in, dumped their coats on the floor, kept their shoes on and raided the kitchen. Bread and jam. No butter. No plates. Made sandwiches on the counter. Left the jam out, lid on the side. Dirty knives on the counter.

Obese bin-bags blistering like blackened boils in the corner.

In the sitting room they flicked the TV on and didn't really watch it. Morning-telly shite. People shouting at each other in front of a room full of people who were encouraging them to get shouty. John rooted through the overflowing ashtray, emptied the last few tokes-worth of tobacco out onto the littered coffee table and pulled a pack of silver king skins from the fruit bowl (which contained keys and pizza flyers and coppers and fluff and dust, but, crucially, no fruit). Bobby handed him a small lump of sticky black tarry shit. John quickly built a bifter. Then they kicked back and sparked up.

Which was how they were sitting when they heard the front door.

Bobby sat bolt-upright in alarm, as he did every time.

John looked at him calmly and said, 'Cal.' As he did every time.

Bobby relaxed.

John then watched the door cautiously for a moment, just in case.

There was some rustling in the hallway, the clatter of something being dropped, and then the noise peeled off into another section of the flat. John's brow furrowed. Cal would usually come through and give him grief. But not this morning. Something must be up. And somewhere deep down John felt let down. Again.

He pushed himself up from the sofa, edged out into the hall and moved stealthily down towards Cal's room. Bobby watched him go with the vaguest interest for the briefest moment before turning back to the telly, his eyes bloodshot and dopey. Cal's door was ajar and John crept up to it, his foot brushing against something on the floor as it went, and he peeped in through the gap. Cal was sat on the end of his bed, trouser leg rolled up, one foot naked, spiking a needle into the skin between his first and second toes. He was doing it left-handed, his right arm resting awkwardly across his other thigh. Cold beads of sweat stood out on his brow.

Cal was sixteen years old. And he was right-handed. He was doing it wrong. Something was wrong. John frowned, stepped closer and pushed the door slightly further open. It creaked.

Cal spun to face his kid brother and looked as if he was gonna say something, shout something, when his eyes widened as his right arm shifted in the course of him turning. He cried out in agony, and John saw that his arm was crooked and loose an inch or two below the elbow. John took a step back and felt his blood run cold. He was squeamish when it came to broken bones and the like. It gave him the fizz to think of them.

'What happened your arm, Cal?'

'Nothing happened,' Cal hissed through clenched teeth.

John looked at his brother. He had no particular feelings for him. He remembered a time when he was much younger when they had played together, but that was ancient history. And it had always been by Cal's rules anyway. There'd never been a time that Cal hadn't bashed him, or shoved him around, taken the toys from his hands and left him wailing – but when they'd been younger... well, they'd been younger, and closer by default. John had been five, maybe six, when his brother had graduated full-time to the streets. More than half a lifetime ago. They were pretty much strangers now.

But John still knew to be cautious of Cal. Thems was the rules. He might be an idiot, like everyone told him, but he wasn't stupid. He looked at his brother then, *really* looked, with the needle sticking out of his foot, nursing his snapped arm, sweating and in agony. Cal was down. And the germ of an idea poked its nose up out of the fertile ground of John's meaner intent.

'Doesn't look like nothing happened to me. Looks fucked to me.'

Cal turned his head to John once again, rage now holding hands with the agony in his eyes. 'You still here? Fuck off.'

John smiled. 'Might. In a minute. Once you've told me what happened your arm.'

'I said fuck off Johnny.'

'You gonna make me?' John smirked gleefully.

Cal's eyes widened at that, and for a moment he had no words. John's smirk broadened into a grin, and something in it caused Cal to frown. He hadn't really noticed his brother for years, other than when he was kicking him to one side to take what he wanted. He noticed him now. He was getting big. And he was starting to look a bit like their dad. Cal remembered their dad. And he was scared of him. But he wasn't scared of John. That would be ridiculous.

He wasn't scared of John.

Ridiculous.

No.

'What's it look like? I fucking broke it, didn't I? Now will you fuck off?'

'I can see you fucking broke it, Cal. I asked *how* you broke it?'

Cal shook his head and screwed up his face. He'd been wracking his brain, ever since that old cunt had snapped his arm like a twig before exploding, to think of how to explain what had happened. But the shock of the injury, coupled with the shock of how he'd sustained it and all the rest, had closed off the whole area of his brain that cooked up the simple lies. The area that his mum had made her own before Dad had left: walked into the door, slipped in the bath, fell down the stairs – that kind of thing.

'Fell down some fucking stairs, alright?'

John narrowed his eyes and considered this for a moment. He didn't buy it.

'Why've you not gone to hospital?'

Because I stabbed an evil old bastard in the park and he snapped my arm and then burst into flames and people might be looking for me is why. He didn't say it. He couldn't believe it. It was all a complete nightmare. And besides, the gear was kicking in now and… just gonna lie down for a minute, just wait for this to take the edge off.

Take all the edges off.

No. Sharp. Edges.

'Just wanted to take some medicine first Johnny, alright? I'll go to the hospital in a bit. Just leave me be, alright?'

John watched his brother sink back into his duvet, his legs still hanging over the foot of the bed. He turned then and went back out into the hall.

Cal was full of shit. Literally.

He kicked something on the floor, and it skittered and glittered along the linoleum ahead of him, catching his eye. He went over, stopped and looked down at it. It lay across the threshold between the hallway and the living room.

'Wha's up with Cal?' Bobby mumbled from a slump on the sofa.

John looked back over his shoulder and saw Cal's hooded coat dumped on the floor inside the front door. Then back down at what lay by his feet. It must have fallen from one of the pockets when Cal had stumbled in.

'He's a cock is what's up with Cal,' Johnny answered distractedly.

'Oh. Yeah.'

John nudged the knife with the toe of his shoe. It was a Stanley knife, blade out two notches. One of the metal-handled efforts. Solid. Weighty. But the blade was tattooed in the most hypnotic way. John squatted down and looked closely at it. The black tiger-stripes burnt into the blade reminded him of the trails raindrops would weave as they fattened and became too heavy to cling to rain-struck windows. He remembered watching the rain on the windows when he was little. He remembered liking it. He remembered when he was little and would sit and watch the rain on the windows for what seemed like hours and he would feel OK. It had made a kind of sense to him that he couldn't put into words, but which made everything else seem acceptable. It made everything seem as if it had its place, even the bad stuff, and that if things got too much, they'd simply roll away under their own weight.

'What the fuck are you doing John?' Bobby was stood right next to him.

John hadn't heard him move.

He'd been somewhere else entirely.

'Nothing.'

He reached down and very carefully picked up the knife, and clicked the blade carefully back into the handle. He didn't want to touch the blade. There was something about it. But he wanted the knife. It was his now.

He pocketed it, went back to the sofa, flopped onto it and dumped his feet up on the coffee table.

'You skinning up or what?'

2

Danny's mother won't be home for an hour or so, but that's OK. He's come to the library with a couple of friends and they're happy enough working their way through pawed copies of *Asterix* and *Tintin*. They share jokes and secrets and laugh quietly, shoulders hunched, careful not to make too much noise. They're good lads. Happy lads. No bother. They should be doing their homework, but hell, sometimes homework can wait.

The time went too quickly this afternoon. There was a lightness to being today that none of then. would have described as such, even if they'd had the vocabulary to do so. No reason. Just was. In spite of the grey, shortening days and chill of looming winter. Perhaps even because of it. Sometimes having no expectations delivers the greatest delights. When friendship and company are easy, and life doesn't make promises and just gets on with simply *living*. This happens only occasionally, and even then mostly only to kids, and usually they grow out of it. They don't even miss it until they become parents themselves, and then it's replaced by a warm sadness that sees them through for the better part of the rest of their lives.

And so a terrible absence of concern; the cruel teeth in the hungry jaws of destiny.

The genetics of tragedy haunting the blood of catastrophe.

So it goes.

Because Danny heads off first. He says goodbye to his friends, takes two *Tintins* and one *Asterix* over to the machine and checks them out. Puts them in his backpack. Leaves the library and then skips guilelessly away into the quickening darkness, towards home.

Mum has told him to get back in good time today. She's doing bolognaise. He loves bolognaise. And they're going to eat it in front of the telly, with the heater on and the lights down low, and they're going to watch *Harry Potter*. The third one. Some of the kids at school say it's weird. But his friends, his *best* friends, say it is the best one.

It's got *werewolves*.

He smiles.

He is ten minutes away from death.

While Danny is checking books out from the library, John and Bobby are stealing alcohol from a newsagent two streets away. It's not the first time, and the guy behind the counter gives chase. They bolt, pulling down a rack of postcards across the door as they go and making good their escape.

They duck sharply left, down the narrow cut-through to the alley that runs behind the main precinct, and then, a few hundred metres further on, they duck left again, through another narrow dink between two buildings and out into a main street one block over, laughing and whooping as they go. The till-jockey from the store having long since given up.

And so, stoned, and hepped-up on adrenaline, they park themselves underneath a graffitied climbing frame in a disused playground and dare each other to down it in one. Which they do. Bang. Super-strength. Tipsy. Like it. Heheheh. Then John pulls a ready-made spliff from the inside pocket of his coat, sparks it and takes a deep pull before passing it across to Bobby. Bobby tugs, coughs, John chuckles, Bobby tugs again, holds it, nods, tugs again, holds it, exhales, leans back, blows a raspberry. And so on. And then they move on. Back into the world, to look for more stuff – more stuff to do, more stuff to take, more stuff to break.

Whatever.

But, as much as they think they are big-men, they are not. They are boys. And there are dangers. And they rarely look out for them.

They wobble out of the playground and back down towards the main thoroughfare – shops and people and stuff. Back towards school. Not ideal, but not a problem: they can duck around behind the library and go that way. And either way, school finished an hour or two ago in any case. Still – there might be teachers hanging around and they're a pain in the arse 24/7. Booky bastards.

They laugh at that and fail to notice a group of older kids fall in behind them.

'Oi! Little John.' One of the older kids calls him out.

John spins on his heel, all laughter evaporating immediately from every cell of his being. He almost sobers up. Almost. He slams his hand into his pocket and takes hold of something, and clicks it a couple of notches. He doesn't bring it out. Not yet.

'Wha…?'

The bigger kids bowl down the street towards them.

'Where's Cal?'

'Dunno.'

'Your brother owes us.'

'I dunno where he is.'

Older kids advancing. John and Bobby inching backward away from them.

Then one of them, the one whose name John knows is Ricky, and whom Cal owes, he stops, narrows his eyes and suggests through drawn lips, 'Well, maybe you can give him a message, yeah?'

John spins and bolts. No hesitation.

He knows that the message would be written in cuts and bruises and has no intention of delivering it. Bobby is slower off the mark and swears in anguish, but pure animal terror gives his step a spring that quickly sees him make up the difference. The older kids give chase. Bobby peels away down a side road, and John heads straight on. He's sprinting for his life, pumping his arms, the knife now out and clenched in his left hand as he runs. The older kids hesitate for a moment at the junction where the younger boys went their separate ways, but it is hesitation enough. A van turns across and in front of them, pulling into the side road, cutting them off. They kick and scream at the van, which screeches to a halt. And suddenly their argument is elsewhere. They have fresh beef.

But John doesn't look back.

He is unaware the chase is now over. His addled, fear-struck, oxygen-hungry mind propels him onwards for two more blocks before a stitch forces him to slow down to a jog. Only then does he dare glance back over his shoulder. He can't see them. He looks again. Still can't see them. He turns then and jogs backward, his eyes darting every which way. And he still can't see them. But he can see Bobby now, chasing to catch up with him.

Which is when Ricky smashes into him from behind.

John screams, flinches down towards the ground, swivels and sticks the knife into his leg. Except it's not Ricky at all.

It's just some kid.

Danny looks at John. John looks back at Danny and is so relieved it's not one of those cunts, he bursts out laughing. It happens so quick, no one even notices. Just kids making a ruckus. Danny looks down at his leg and then back up at John.

It hurts.

He hopes it doesn't make him late for bolognaise.

Or Harry Potter.

It's got werewolves.

John clicks the blade back into the handle and pockets the knife without thinking.

'Fuck sake, John… Jesus…' Bobby gasping for breath. 'Lost 'em ages ago.'

Bobby then sees the little kid stood there regarding them, a weird look in his eyes. 'What the fuck are you looking at?' and he shoves him. Danny goes quietly down. Then they leave him there, skipping away into the shadows, laughing and whooping, kicking cans and spitting.

And for a moment, no one comes to Danny. For just a moment he is alone.

No bolognaise for Danny tonight. No.

No nothing for Danny tonight. But these thoughts can't be his. They must be lies.

He refocuses.

Gotta get home.

Dinner ready soon.

Leg hurts.

Mummy fix it.

Harry Potter.

Werewolves.

Asterix and *Tintin*.

A homeless person then emerges from the shadows and cautiously approaches him. Takes the measure of him. But Danny is elsewhere.

Harry and werewolves and *Asterix* and *Tintin*.

The tramp pulls rags tight over his face, his hood down low. He sidles over to Danny and leans down and, taking the child's face in his hands says, 'Look at me, child.'

The child's face turns, but it is not the child that speaks. It is something other, something older. Its eyes are paler, its soul darker. It looks up at the tramp and says, 'Take your scum hands off me, rat-filth.'

And the tramp lets him go. Lowers him back down to the ground. And he backs quickly away. The tramp turns and heads away into the early-evening darkness and leaves Danny on the ground.

Danny then rallies. The flight receptors in his brain now firing on all cylinders, granting him one last measure of light before the closing of the curtains. He is just yards from the stairs up to the flat. Just minutes from home. Minutes from bolognaise and *Harry Potter* and Mummy fixing his leg. *Minutes.*

His leg feels funny. It doesn't even hurt. Except it kind of hurts more than anything he's ever felt in his whole life. A pain so vast and so absolute he can't find its edges and so can't properly take it in. And, swimming in the blanketing darkness of that pain, there is a creature. He can see it there, circling. It thinks he can't see it. But he can. But he knows if he ignores it, then it won't catch him.

Because he's got the answers that'll fix this situation.

He's got bolognaise and *Harry Potter*.

He's got *Asterix* and *Tintin*.

He's got stairwell and strangers and holding his hand and he'll be OK and fading away and swimming out into the void. He goes carefully. Because he knows something's out there. Swimming. Looking for something to eat.

And it's not werewolves.

It's not werewolves…

It's not…

It's…

3

Danny was already dead when they wheeled him in.

It was 5.32 p.m.

The wound on his leg had been staunched in the ambulance, but he'd bled too much and his heart had already given up. It had given up before the paramedics had even got to him. But it would've been rude not to try. So they'd patched his leg and hammered his chest. Zapped him a couple of times too. They'd all read stories. Watched films.

Sometimes they came back.

Usually they didn't.

This time, he hadn't.

He was ten years old.

He'd been found in a stairwell in a forest of concrete, in a place that smelt of piss. He had nearly made it home, where he thought he'd be safe.

He hadn't made it.

Wouldn't have changed anything if he had.

The builders who had found him had tied some cord round his upper thigh and had succeeded in delaying the inevitable. One of them had held his hand and had told him to hold on. They would all remember the look in the boy's eyes as he'd died. Wide eyes. Scared, yes, but never aware that it was over. His eyes had said, 'It'll be OK', all the way up to the edge. Then they had dilated and glazed over as he'd gone over the drop and into the darkness. The builders would remember that. And it would keep them up at night.

For a while.

The paramedics had radioed ahead and wheeled him straight into one of the furthest-flung assessment rooms. One of the rooms that rarely saw any degree of actual treatment. These were the rooms where they wheeled the dead. And the very-soon-to-be-dead. Out of the way. A facilities manager had once produced a traffic-flow report and had advised that these rooms were the rooms to which any volume of footfall would cause the most amount of disruption to the unit as a whole. And so they'd been set aside for those that needed the least attention. And those had been the dead, and the sure-to-be-dying. The rooms constituted a cursed appendix to the body of the A&E department. A glottal stop between here and the morgue.

Danny lay there, dead, and he waited.

After the paramedics and the doctors and an initial burst of morbid professional interest and activity, a nurse had come in and looked at him and checked his pulse and scribbled on his notes. She had looked at his face and had felt sad. He looked like a nice boy. But then they always did when they were dead.

She had wondered where his parents were.

There'd be a call at some point.

From the police. But not until later. Once they'd called, his family – once they'd made the call. Reported him missing.

They'd apologise for probably wasting their time. They always did.

The parents always stalled before calling the police, worried. As if they thought calling the police with their concerns would somehow transmute terrified imagination into appalling reality. Turn gold into lead. An inverted alchemy. And tonight, that call would do just that.

The nurse hoped that his parents left it as long as they could bear. That they would prolong their anger – 'Why hasn't he called!' – and then savour their fear – 'OK, if you hear from him, could you let us know' – because as soon as they made *that* call, it would be over. They would be parents no more. Even if he had siblings, they would be parents no more. They would become something else. Not parents living the dream, but just people with children who now truly understood the abyss over which they teetered. Because they'd be falling into it, and would be evermore.

And their boy would be dead.

She looks at him, and shakes her head. Then she pulls the sheet up and over his face, hangs the notes back on the end of the bed and pads out of the room.

The door swishes quietly closed behind her.

And the boy sits up.

The sheet falls away and his eyes open.

They are pale. Blue irises. They'd been brown, like his skin, when he'd died. But now they are pale, as is his skin without blood. He has changed.

He pushes the sheet down and kicks his feet free.

His school trousers are charcoal-grey. But they are black, and damp, round a mean, clean tear on the inside of his upper-right thigh. He swings his legs round and hangs his feet over the edge of the bed.

He sways a little.

He holds on to the edge of the mattress with both hands and closes his eyes.

Then he unfastens the trousers, kicks off his school shoes and pushes the trousers down and off. He raises them and turns the stain to his face, balls them up and pushes his open, thirsty mouth into the wet fabric and sucks. He gets a taste, the slightest quenching, then turns the trousers to seek more blood. He does this over and over and over again, until he is satisfied that he has taken as much as they have to offer.

Then he puts the trousers down on the bed beside him. His face now wears crimson round his mouth and across his cheeks like a clown who's been punched. He looks at the wound on his thigh. It has been sutured, and it is smaller than one might expect, but a part of him, a new part of him, one that wasn't there before, understands just how unimpressive a fatal wound can be. How *narrow* the exit can be for life to depart a body.

And it is this part of him, this new part, which whispers to him and tells him he must leave.

So he pulls his trousers back on, drops down from the bed. He wobbles – he is still far too thirsty – no longer faint, but still some way from stable on his feet. He leans against the bed and wheedles his feet back into his shoes. The back of his left shoe folds in under his heel, and he hikes it out deftly with the forefinger of his right hand.

He moves to the door, leans in against it and listens.

There's a whole bunch of hubbub out there, but that might work in his favour.

He pulls the door open a crack and peeps out into the glare.

To the left, looking across the width of the door and past the hinges, lies the tumult and bedlam of the A&E department. No escape that way.

He scans the hallway, looking for one of the green signs that indicate which way to bolt when the place goes up in flames. Green sign, picture of a white door with a green stickman running through it. An arrow and two words: Fire Exit.

When he finds it, it points the way he'd hoped. Away from the hubbub. As well it might. Back past the door to his room and away.

He ducks out without hesitation and walks away from A&E. He doesn't look back. Seconds later he is through a double set of swing doors and into a lightless corridor. Lightless apart from a green light ahead. Another arrow. Another set of swing doors. These lead out into a stairwell and the breadcrumb trail of green signs guides him down two storeys to a final set of doors. These doors are closed and a last, red sign warns that they are alarmed.

Once again, he doesn't hesitate. He smashes through the doors and darts quickly across the narrow drive at the back of the building and into the multi-storey car park opposite.

A siren starts to bleat and there is a sudden flurry of almost activity. People stop and look around. They look at each other and shrug their shoulders. They look for someone to tell them what to think, what to do. Is this a drill? What?

The boy finds a shadow in which to lurk and observe the indecision play out. A security guard approaches the open fire escape from the outside. The guard looks left, then right, then left again. Then he speaks into his radio, steps through the door and pulls it closed behind him. A few moments later the alarm falls silent.

The absence of relief is as omnipresent as was the absence of concern.

And the world trundles on.

The boy ducks deeper into the car park, bolting at a crouch between cars parked bumper to bumper. The neon lights running in strips down the aisle occasionally stab at his newly sensitised eyes. The smell of lead and monoxide turns his stomach.

Into another stairwell and up to the roof. He needs to get his bearings.

Up and up, until he is out and beneath the orange-hued nightscape, a very few of the brightest stars peeping meekly through the torn blanket of grizzly cloud. It is a cold and cruddy night.

He walks to the furthest corner on this highest level and peers out across the city. His vision is keen, honed. Hawk-like. To most the towers of the poisoned vista laid out before him would be a smorgasbord of indistinguishable concrete hutches. But to him, this boy, this dead boy, with something old now very much alive within him, they all look different. They all speak to him. They each sing their own song of despair.

He prowls the rooftop, looking and hearing and *feeling*, searching for the beacon that will tell him where to go.

Because out there, somewhere, behind one of those count-less, dead-eyed windows, someone is looking back at him. And that someone is the other half of him.

And he needs to find him before he splits again.

CHAPTER FOUR

MERGERS AND ACQUISITIONS

1

I stand outside the door and wait. I am also on the inside of the door struggling to reach for the lock to let myself in. The me inside is too short, so I summon the dog.

It skiffles down the hallway, struggling now. I'm not a good fit for it. I am too much. The lower animals quickly fall apart when my kind adopt them. And I've allowed the child to snack on him – just enough to keep the boy going so that we can do what needs doing here. But the dog is weakening. It will probably serve me – *us* – for a few more hours before it collapses. It will be enough. It will have to be.

I have the dog crouch down and allow the child to sit astride his back just below his stocky shoulders. Then I have the dog stand. His legs shaking a little with the extra weight of the child. He gets breathless quickly. Within the confines of his tiny mind he pines for release and is consumed by primal fear. He's too dumb to understand his situation, other than to know that he has been caught in the jaws of a predator much larger than himself.

He lifts the child up, and I have the boy push himself upright, leaning against the wall and the door for balance. He tiptoes and reaches for the lock. Unlike the dog, the child seems positively brimming with life. Eager to learn. Desperate to impress. He takes my hand, in here, as if he's been waiting his whole life for me, and now that I'm here he will do anything.

That he will do as he's told is enough.

He flicks the lock, and I push the door open from the outside. It swings open and the older boy, the one I have brought here from the hospital, the one who so ably shoplifted a few items for the little one en route, puts his arms round the baby and lifts him gently to the floor.

The older child is more complicated than the younger one. He doesn't take my hand. But he understands he should be dead, and were it not for me then he would be. He is consumed by something new and profound, something which he has never tasted before in his young, innocent life. He doesn't much care for the taste of it yet, but he seems compelled to keep taking sips. It is anger. Rage, in fact. But it is muddled with childish images of dog-men, and rat-food, and his being denied these simple things. These things I don't understand. He is a ball of confusion and wayward emotion, like a pupating caterpillar about to emerge as something new. He went in as a child. He will emerge as, well... he will emerge as something more like myself. So, for now, he is wary of me, but our purpose is common enough that we can share it and he is happy enough to work with me. He wants the child that stuck the knife in his leg. I want the knife.

I send the dog back to the threshold of the living room to continue his observance of the rats that remain unconscious in their pit, bathing in dirty opiate dreams beneath the sickly glow of their TV and its looping images of rutting vermin.

We head through to the child's disgusting nest, with its flyblown curtains and the landfill scraps the child thinks of as his toys. All of them dead. All of them decaying. We go through quietly. We have some preparations to make.

I have the older child empty out the small cloth bag he has brought with him onto the mattress. The bag itself was lifted from the same charity shop as the cheap polyester wedding suit and shirt that fall from it: 18–24 months. Peter is small for his age, undernourished, so it might be a little baggy. We'll see. A pair of hairdresser's scissors also drops out, and a packet of disposable razors. Two ten-metre reels of nylon cord. And the last thing: some shower gel.

I take the scissors in my older hands and turn to the younger me, and we snip away at the unruly blond locks that are teaming with lice, fattened and herding. I dispose of the hair in the toy box, where it will later burn, along with anything else that needs disposing of. Once most of the hair is gone, I turn the child to look at me. He smiles, and I smile back.

His smile is his, his own, not mine.

And my smile is mine, my own, writ large across the face of the older child.

We hold like that for a moment. We neither of us expected it. And yet here it is.

The older child doesn't join in. He's not in the mood. And he wants to get on with it.

I nod, for all of us, take the shampoo and the razors in one of Danny's hands, and the little one's hand in the other before leading them through to the bathroom and closing the door behind us.

The dog continues his watch.

It is as filthy in here as it is everywhere else. I help the little one into the bath, remove his stained vest and saturated nappy. The older child baulks somewhat at the little one's filth, but he endures it stoically and helps get the job done. We attach the short rubber shower-adapter to the taps and run the water as quietly as possible, mostly cold with just a dash enough of warm so as not to actually hurt. Then we hose him down. Inside, in here, with us, he squeals and complains, but without much conviction. This is new to him and he doesn't like it, but a better part of him appreciates it.

We shampoo his whole body, including his head. Especially his head. Then we take a razor from the packet and carefully shave his scalp. We take the top off a couple of louse bites and the scent of his blood drives us all crazy. But we contain ourselves. Then we rinse him down and lift him out. The only towel we have to dry him with is musty, stiff and scratchy but it will do.

Back in the bedroom we put him in his suit. No nappy. He won't be needing one any more. Not as long as he has me, and he has me until this is done. Once he is ready we stand back and look at him. He gives us a twirl. The older child smiles at that. His first smile this side of death. He enjoys it.

Then we send Peter through with two words: *get her*.

He marches off proudly, but quietly. The older child lies down and closes his eyes and allows my focus to stay with Peter. So I toddle down the hall. The dog glances over its shoulder at me as I approach. The next few minutes are the most open to possible deviation from the carefully plotted course. Ideally we can extract the mother without waking the man-rat. It all depends on her.

Peter and I gently order the dog to his feet. He stands, wearily, and we send him into the room while we wait in the doorway to oversee things. The male is sprawled across the armchair, asleep. Drug sleep. There is a nervous twitch ticking away in the wrist of his right hand. A sleeping dog who, for the time being, we would prefer to let lie.

The dog moves closer to the mother and pushes his muzzle into her face and snuffles and licks. She pushes him away and rolls away from him. The dog perseveres, nibbles at her ear. Tugs at her hair. She rolls back and her eyes half open. She goes to smack the dog, but all intent escapes her when she sees the child, shaved and suited, at the foot of the sofa beyond the beast. Her face forms the dumb sign for question, and I have the child speak. 'Mother. Please. Come with me.'

It is the longest sentence he has ever spoken.

Then the dog backs away and the boy waves for her to follow.

She pushes herself half upright and watches him go, gormless disbelief honking silently from her face.

Once the dog has backed out from between the coffee table and the sofa, he turns and pads weakly out of the room. 'Come along Mother,' the child trills.

I then open the eyes of the older child and ready him in the room.

The dog and Peter come through first. Peter turns and waits for her.

She shambles in after him.

Peter looks up at her and says, 'Mama.'

She leans down to touch his naked scalp and says, 'What happened your...?'

Peter springs then, wraps his arms round her neck and swings into her arms. I have Danny leap at the same time, onto her back and reaching round, covering her mouth and clamping it shut. Peter then sinks his teeth into the doughy flesh that covers her collarbone and takes a sip. She tries to shake us off, but stumbles and goes down. She tries to scream, tries to breathe, and flails and flaps.

And then I'm ripped apart again – this time intentionally – and I'm in, and she is mine, and it is done.

We lie there, the three of us, the three of me, wrapped round each other for a short moment and we simply exist. The moment is almost post-coital.

Once we have caught our breath, I get her up and set her to work, and allow Peter and Danny to rest. I take her through to the sty that she calls her bedroom and have her root around until she has found a belt. We then head quietly back into the living room and investigate the man-rat. The female is surer of the depth of his unconsciousness than I am. She seems confident that we can bind him and that he will remain out. That he would in fact remain out if the world were to end. I believe her.

So we hoist him upright, cross his arms in his lap, throw the belt round his wrists, pull it tight and then tie it in a knot at the buckle. Then we take one of the reels of nylon cord from the back pocket of our dirty tracksuit bottoms, wind it round him once, tie another knot, then wind it round him four or five times more, tie it tight, then snip off what's left with the hairdressing scissors. Then we bind his feet.

Once he is bound we have Danny come through and tie her up on the sofa – all for show, of course – and then Danny heads back through, and the mother lies there and waits for him to wake up.

And once he is awake, we will work together to ensure that he will fear us, because then he will do what we need him to do. He will help us find the one with the knife, the one with the broken arm. And then we shall start putting things right.

2

When Ste came to, when he surfaced from the brown haze, Donna was whining and his hands were tied behind him.

He was bound to the chair in which he'd passed out that morning.

'Wha…?'

He scanned the room and found it much as he recalled leaving it. There was a bag of gear on the table, all his kit. Telly was still there. He'd not been robbed.

Donna was tied up too. She was prone on the sofa, weeping and whimpering. She wasn't secured to anything, not as Ste was to the chair, but nor was she making any attempt to escape.

Ste wasn't scared. He was angry. Always his first recourse. He thrashed in his chair, but to no avail.

'What the fuck's goin' on, Don?'

Her head snapped to face him and she sobbed, panicking. 'Don't know Ste… think it musta been a bad batch… don't make no sense…' She was gulping for air between each spoken clause, hysterical drama-school crying.

Ste just frowned at her like an idiot. He didn't even ask her what the fuck she was talking about. It went without saying. It always did.

'Well are you just gonna just lie there like a fat cunt or are you gonna come over here and help untie me?'

'I *can't*…' she wheezed desperately, '… he's got Petey and said if I moved he'd… he'd…'

'Said he'd *what*? *Who* said?' Ste decided right then that the second he got loose he was gonna beat the living shit out of the stupid bitch.

'*I* said if she moved, I'd cut the boy's head off and put it back where it came from.'

For the briefest of moments Ste was dumbstruck: there was a nigger-child in the shadow of the doorway, tipping his head to indicate Donna's groin as the place he had threatened to shove Petey's head.

Then the dumbstruck moment passed, and Ste laughed.

'Go on then. Little cunt would probably love it up there, hey, Don?' Ste sniggered at his own wit and grinned. Then the grin disappeared and the anger returned. 'Fuck's sake Donna, get off the fucken sofa and get over here. It's just a kid, what the fuck's he gonna…?'

'No Ste, don't, you don't…' she whispered. She wouldn't even look at the child.

'She's quite right, Steven, you don't understand. And nor, in all likelihood, will you ever. But that's neither here nor there. I came here for something and I intend to get it. And you will help me.'

The incongruity of the child's sing-song pre-teen voice and his older, dustier words was entirely lost on Ste. He thrust forward in his chair and hissed, 'You can go fuck yourself you nigger piece of shit and when I get out of this I'm going to fuck your arse and then I'm going to fucking kill you…'

The child then moved so quickly, and so silently, it was as if he were smoke. In the blinking of an eye he was face to face with Ste. The pale-blueness of his eyes was wrong. The pallor of his skin was wrong. Something about his teeth when he smiled – wrong. But Ste managed to push most of that to one side. Whatever may or may not have been wrong, or right, this was still just a nigger-child in his home, threatening him.

Ste spat in his face.

The child's smile broadened and his arm moved in a blur to one side. There was a short, sharp ripping sound, like Velcro being unfastened. The child held Ste's gaze, eyeball to eyeball, and Ste found himself strangely transfixed. Even when the heat, swiftly followed by the pain, bloomed on the side of his head.

The child held up something for Ste to see and released him from his hypnotic gaze. Ste couldn't immediately make out what it was he was looking at. His face was a mask of combined confusion and rapidly amplifying agony.

'Your ear, rat. I don't think you'll be fucking my, or anyone else's, arse anytime soon. Nor do I think it'll be *you* killing *me*. What say you?'

Donna turned away from the whole scene, and curled into as close to a ball as she could. She made a curious, reedy, whistling noise. The child looked at her, then back at Ste. Then he turned and moved back across the room to sit in the seat opposite Ste. He dropped the ear on the table as he went.

'I say fuck you,' Ste managed to sigh through the excruciating pain he now endured. He said it, but the words lacked bite this time. They were a lie. Front. But it wasn't just the pain that had quieted him. He was now afflicted by uncertainty. Doubt. Something he hadn't tasted since he was a smaller man than the litany of so-called fathers his mother had foisted on him in his youth.

'I'm sure you do. I'm sure you do.' The child exhaled melodramatically. 'Perhaps a little more persuasion needed, then.'

Ste slumped back in his chair, an over-engineered expression of insouciance on his face, feigned disinterest. But not feigned enough. His fingers picked and fidgeted at each other. He looked at the child in the chair opposite, who in turn looked towards the door and trilled two words: 'Here boy.'

There then followed the sound of movement from Peter's bedroom. Ste turned to watch the doorway, and Donna peeped out from her flinch position too. They heard the dog padding across the boy's room, out into the hall and towards the doorway. When he crossed the threshold into the room Donna moaned, and Ste gasped.

The dog's eyes were glazed and open at half-mast. He had tiny baby bite marks intermittently pocking his hide, and dried blood had woven trails in tendrils across his coat. And sat astride him, squeaky-clean and wearing brand-new clothes – a little wedding suit, white socks – his head shaved and a crimson clown's mouth smeared across his lips, was Peter. He looked malevolently at his mother, and then at Ste. Then he looked at the older child, and they both smirked at each other. Quite the jolly prank.

'Down boy,' commanded the older child, and the dog obeyed, his ears pulled back in terror that was now innate. The dog looked across at Ste, his dull eyes conveying everything that needed conveyance – the beast had been bested and the kids were in control.

Peter swung his leg up and over the dog's back and dismounted with a cruel flourish. Peter and the other child's smirks both broadened simultaneously – they were enjoying this, but they seemed not to be a 'they'. They seemed as one.

Ste pushed himself back into his chair and fell utterly silent, rapt and unmoored by the scene playing out before him. Peter pranced across the room to the older child and leant in to whisper something in his ear. The older child grinned and swivelled his eyes to Ste as he did so. He nodded and licked his lips.

Peter then held his chubby little baby hands up to his mouth and chuckled bashfully. It should have sounded innocent, but the blood on his face, and the outfit, made it the absolute opposite. It sounded terrible, and Ste wanted to cover his ears.

His *ear*.

Then Peter saw something on the table before him and abruptly ceased his giggling. The other child followed his gaze, raised an eyebrow and said, 'Go on then.' The baby scuttled across the room, seized the ear from where it had been discarded and put it to his lips. He hummed as he chewed and gnawed at what little could be wrung from the scrap. But he was still thirsty when he was done, and he started to bleat.

'Hush now. There's plenty more where that came from,' consoled the older child. Both children turned to look at Ste.

Ste's eyes widened, understanding now. And believing. All front dissipated. 'No. Oh god, no. Please. Take her…' He nodded towards Donna, who now did nothing but shiver on the sofa, 'Take her.'

'Stop your squealing, rat. We'll take what we want, when we want it,' the older child intoned. He looked at Peter and then the dog. Peter heeded a wordless instruction and turned away from Ste and his mother, went back to the dog, lay down on the floor beside it, put his mouth to his belly, bit down – the dog squeaked feebly but made no move to resist – and the child suckled.

It sounded like the end of a milkshake being pulled through a straw.

Ste sobbed. 'What the fuck is going on? This can't be happening...' His face crumpled, and he collapsed into himself. He became the child he'd once been before other kinds of monsters had turned him into the monster he'd become – and he cried, and feared, much as he had done back then.

'Shhhh, rat. Hush now. No need for tears. We don't need you for *that*.' He tipped his head back at the baby as he fed. 'No. I can think of no chalice more toxic.' The child shuddered his distaste at the very notion. 'All I need from you is one small thing.'

'What? Anything!'

'Anything?'

'Yes... anything...'

'Good.'

The child picked up Ste's mobile from the littered table. He studied it, fiddled with it and then held it up in front of Ste. Ste looked at it – the small screen read 'Cal' – then back at the child, and didn't understand. The child looked hard into Ste's eyes, shook the phone in his face, pointed assertively at the floor and said two words: 'Summon him.'

'OK,' Ste nodded, 'OK, I'll do it.'

'Good rat... good rat...'

And then Ste did what he had to do.

3

The world swims back into weak focus to the shrill, repetitive strains of his mobile phone. It squalls at him, and vibrates weakly from his pocket. His eyes slowly open and he looks up at the ceiling, bathed in the prickly afterglow of the drugs. With the soothing opiate high tide now quickly receding, he can sense the shingle of his arm's agony lurking there in the shallows, waiting to pounce and consume him once again.

He lets the call go to voicemail.

With every breath he takes the tide recedes further, the pain screams louder, the shingle ripping and roaring with every retreating wave, and the clarity of his world sharpens in every way. And that clarity also presages a shattering confusion and broadening sense of disbelief. The old fucker on the bench, the knife, the fire.

His arm.

It doesn't make sense.

Nightmare.

But here he is, lying on his bed, bracing himself for the full subsonic glory of his agony to swoop back in. Waiting for the drop. He's going to need more drugs.

His phone goes off again.

He almost reaches for it with his bad arm, but remembers just in time. He's starting to get used to it now, that's how much the insane truth of the last twenty-four hours is starting to sink in. He reaches across himself with his good arm and awkwardly fishes the phone from his pocket. He examines the screen before answering it: Ste.

He frowns. Ste never calls him. But he answers it nonetheless.

He listens to what Ste has to say.

'Really?'

What Ste has to say is the last thing he might ever have expected.

So unexpected, and so *welcome*, that he fails to notice the peculiarity of the peripheral detail. Ste has just told him that he left his gear round at Ste's place, and did he want to pop back and get it? Oh, and could he bring the knife. Pete's had an allergic reaction and the doctors might need to just do a quick test. Tetanus and whatnot. Y'know?

'Yeah yeah. OK. I'll be there in a bit.'

And then he is gone.

And the waves pull back and the shingle roars and Cal moans in distress. He pushes himself carefully upright, but all the care in the world doesn't blunt the fangs of it. He looks down at the floor by his feet. One foot naked, the other still socked and shoed. A needle lies on the floor just by the bare foot, and a couple of spots of congealed blood dot the carpet in between. His baggy of gear is there too. Couple of shots left. Good. He's going to need them.

His baggy's here?

But Ste said…

Cal pauses and thinks then.

Ste said he'd left his gear round his. Ste must be fucked. Cal smiles. It's not often that people fuck up in his favour. But it had to happen at some point.

Maths isn't it, you stupid cunt?

That's what his dad always used to say, usually just before he smashed the shit out of something. Or someone. Cal had never understood what he'd meant. Still didn't.

Cal thinks about shooting up quickly now, his arm screams out for it, but then he reconsiders. It'd only slow him down and opportunity might give up knocking – he could be back at Ste's in fifteen minutes, his arm would survive and he could shoot up then and be a baggy up on what he's got right now. It is as close to thinking beyond the short term as he has managed in quite some years.

He struggles to pull his sock back on, stuffs his foot into his shoe and pushes himself upright. There is a fresh cold sweat breaking out across his brow. The pain in his arm is plateauing now at a howling juggernaut of all-consuming noise, its very constancy making it somehow easier to bear – when it comes in waves, it is the peaks that really twist the knife; but now the tide is out and the rocky shore fully exposed all the time, it is easier to endure. It doesn't thud and throb now. It doesn't ease then ROAR, ease then ROAR, ease then ROAR. Now it just ROARS. Job done. Game over. And he can move on.

In the hallway he leans down, grabs his coat and gingerly eases it on. His keys are in the pocket. He leaves the flat and makes it halfway down to the ground floor before he remembers the knife. He stops, considers going on without it, then figures against: a once-in-a-lifetime opportunity and he doesn't want to run the risk of blowing it.

He drags himself back up to the flat, lets himself in and then hesitates again. Where the fuck is it anyway? Hadn't it been in his coat? He double-checks his pockets. Not there. He scans the floor around the inside of the front door. There is a pile of crap strewn there, but no knife. Had he put it down somewhere? He can't even remember getting back to the flat. He closes his eyes and forces his memory to give him something to work with. No. He'd got in, dropped his coat on the floor and headed straight into his room and cooked up. What then?

John.

John had come in.

What had he said?

Just asked about his arm. Hadn't he? He was pretty sure that was it. The memory was vague at best. His father was threatening to intrude upon the scene as it replayed behind the fusty curtains of his conscious mind. And that made no sense. But no. He couldn't join the dots. He might even have lost it before he got back to the flat in the first place.

Fuck it. He'd just have to explain it to Ste. Doctors can do blood tests and shit anyway, couldn't they? What the fuck did they need the knife for? The more he thinks about it, the less sense it makes, the less it matters. He leaves the flat again, his mind chewing over questions that are starting to raise their voices: where was the knife? Why did Ste really need it? When did Ste start giving a fuck about Pete anyway? Wasn't he always kicking the shit out of him as it was? Christ, hadn't Cal even seen him set the dog on the poor little bastard, laughing, making like it was the funniest fucking thing he'd ever seen?

And how fucked must he be to think a bag of gear in his flat was anyone's but his own? And then to think it was Cal's? And then to phone Cal and tell him to pop round and get it?

Cal stops in his tracks then and almost makes the smartest decision of his life. He doesn't know the phrase 'honeytrap', doesn't even really know the concept, but all of these questions outline a not dissimilar notion now trying to solidify in his roiling mind. The notion very nearly changes the course of things. But then the scent of the honey lures more strongly, and insinuates other factors to counter the truth that he's almost exposed.

What else could Ste want? Cal doesn't owe *him* money. He hasn't robbed him. Hasn't even robbed anyone Ste knows. And now that he's thought about it, he really *doesn't* have enough gear left. He does need some more. So even if he doesn't end up getting the baggy for free after all, he can still tick another one and he'll be OK until the morning. Then maybe he can take his arm to hospital and tell them he fell down some stairs like he probably should've done in the first place. He just needs to calm his fucking nerves. He's sketching out like a bastard and another baggy and a bit more sleep and everything will be alright. And maybe he can start sorting his shit out tomorrow. Maybe he can even think about kicking the habit tomorrow.

Yeah. That's what he'll do. Go to Ste's, see what the fuck's going on, get the free baggy, or tick one, whatever, go home, jack up and deal with everything tomorrow. Sorted.

At Ste's he knocks on the door. He doesn't bang this time. He's in too much pain and too exhausted and doesn't have enough adrenaline pumping around his system. He hears footsteps coming down the hallway. The door opens. It's Donna.

It's never Donna.

She simply lets the door swing open and plods back down the hallway into the sitting room. Cal hesitates yet again, and then follows her in. The place has a funny smell to it. It always smells like shit and old sweat in here, and it still does, but there's another, unfamiliar smell marbling it. A clean smell. Shampoo?

Really?

No matter.

He passes Pete's room and the door is closed fully. It's never closed fully. So is the bathroom door opposite. All of these little things. But none of them enough.

He walks into the sitting room and freezes. There's a little black boy, wearing a school uniform, sitting in Ste's chair, looking at him. Donna is sat upright on the sofa, hands folded in her lap, looking at him. And between them, sat astride the dog, wearing a little wedding suit, head shaved, is Peter. Looking at him.

The TV isn't on.

Everything is wrong.

'Where… where's Ste?' Cal stammers feebly.

'Ste's gone, rat,' reply all three people in the room in unison, their voice in harmony with another, deeper voice behind him in the hall.

Cal's eyes widen in terror, and he spins on his heel to see Ste coming at him, fist raised, swinging down. It smooshes Cal's nose and his legs sit him down on the floor.

The black kid, Donna, Peter and Ste – even the dog – all swivel their heads and watch him go down. The last thing he sees before his eyes flutter and he blacks out.

'We need to talk, rat,' they all trill in hellish harmony. The last thing he hears.

Then he's adrift in a darkness that will be the last moment of peace he will experience before the final dash to his appalling death.

4

Cal came to in the armchair. His nose smarted and there was blood painted in a stripe from his upper lip, down across his mouth and chin. He wasn't restrained, but he had no particular urge to move, not confronted with what he was confronted with.

Sat about the room, looking at him, were all of them – Ste and Donna, Peter and the dog and the black kiddy. The sofa had been pulled across the door to the hallway, and everyone but Ste was on it. Ste was in his chair.

They sat there and regarded at him with curiously dislocated expressions on their faces. Well, Donna and Ste anyway. The kids looked fearsomely alive and present. Peter looked like no child Cal had ever seen before, but especially unlike the tiny mite that used to lurk in the corners whenever Cal came round here.

Ste leant forward then, awkwardly, as if shoved, and said, 'Would you like to take some drugs now, rat? It might help you through what happens next. I won't be offering again.'

Cal flinched at that. His arm was howling louder than ever, and his face wasn't far behind it, and he'd love nothing more than a good hit. But the way Ste had spoken. The words he'd used. They weren't Ste. Ste had never spoken to him like that. Ste had barely actually ever spoken to him at all, other than to do business. And he had certainly never called him…

'Rat…? Did you call me rat?' The old-one? From the park? But how…?'

'Oh, I'm sorry…' began Ste.

'… would you prefer it if I…' continued Donna.

'… called you something else…' chimed in the older child.

'… like, perhaps, *vermin*?' concluded Peter.

The dog nodded.

Then they all chuckled the same malignant chuckle.

Cal pushed himself back into the chair then and started to shake his head. This had to be the final straw. Please god, let this be it now. The nightmare that was today kept getting worse and worse, and he couldn't take any more. He wanted to wake up now. But he was already awake. 'What the fuck? What the fuck?' he trailed off into a failed attempt at repressed weeping. His blocked nose didn't help, his sobs expressed themselves fully through his mouth and there was some dribbling involved. It wasn't pretty.

Peter hopped down from the sofa then and went across to Cal, reached out, took his hand and spoke to him in his lilting baby voice, his pretty blue eyes wide and sincere. 'OK, rat, OK. I'll give you one last chance: would you like to take some drugs? I think it might be best if you do.'

Cal held on to Peter's hand and looked at the little boy. 'Why?' he wailed. 'What are you going to do to me?' Then he continued hopelessly, 'I'm sorry. I wasn't really going to stick you, but when you grabbed my arm it hurt so bad I just did it, y'know, it just happened, it wasn't my fault…'

'Of course it wasn't your fault,' answered the older child coldly, one finger idly fiddling with a small tear on the inside leg of his trousers as he spoke. 'It never is your fault. These things just happen. You just *happened* to get into trouble. You just *happened* to be carrying a weapon. You just *happened* to use it. Of course you didn't mean to. Where is the knife now, rat? You were asked to bring it.'

'I don't know where it is… it's gone…'

'And where do you suppose you lost it?'

'I don't fucking know, do I? I had other things on my mind. Fuck off.' He bawled these words pleadingly. They had no weight.

'Ahh… there he is… there's the rat I remember,' they all intoned darkly. 'Perhaps if I describe someone to you, you might be able to help me with my enquiries,' continued the older child. 'You see I – well, I say "I", I mean Danny here–' he patted his chest to indicate he was talking about himself, the black boy, 'was making his way home from the library, minding his own business, when another boy ran into him, turned round and stuck your knife into his leg.' Danny stood then and showed Cal where the knife had gone through his trousers and into his leg. 'See? He did that, and then I was in him, as well as young Peter here, who also cut himself on your knife. I've not been dragged into anyone else since then, so I can only assume that the same boy that attacked Danny here still has the knife. I need to find him.'

'OK... OK...' Cal nodded feebly.

'He had hair much like yours. He was younger than you, but older than Danny. Maybe a year or two older. He was wearing school clothes under a large... bomber jacket is it? No... ski coat... like a quilt?' Danny looked as if he was having a conversation with himself internally, then he continued, 'Oh, and he had a friend. Red hair. Curly. Freckles.'

Cal's eyes widened ever so slightly at that.

Danny tilted his head, 'And the redhead said his name: he called him John. You know who it is, don't you, rat?'

Cal shook his head and lied. Badly.

'You do know, of course, that there are other ways that I can get the information if I have to. I could just climb in there and take it.' Danny nodded towards Ste and Donna, who both looked at Cal, and who were both for the briefest of moments allowed to express themselves. And what they expressed was a sheer wall of confused terror, of being possessed, inhabited. Plagued. And then they were gone again, buried, and the dislocated absence was once more back in their place.

Cal hesitated, but not for any worthwhile amount of time. 'OK, OK, I'll tell you... but you gotta promise not to hurt him...'

'I have to promise no such thing, rat...' – again, all of them – '... you will tell me now, or I will climb into your wretched little carapace and rip the information out of your worthless excuse of a soul. Then I will devour you and everyone who has anything to do with you, until I get what I want. Do you understand me?'

Cal turned away from them, buried his face in the chair and wailed.

Peter then continued, 'Or you could just tell me, Cal, and the fate of the child will be in his own hands. If he proffers the knife without resistance, then I see no reason for him to come to any harm.'

Danny flinched ever so slightly at that. Peter glanced briefly across at him and narrowed his eyes authoritatively. Cal missed this exchange, and gave in. 'Alright. John's my kid brother. He must've nicked it from my coat or something when I got in this morning.'

'Where can I find him?'

'Fuck knows… he's never in until late… he just fucks about out all day, innit?'

Peter sighed with exasperation. 'Where do *you* live, Cal? What's your address? He lives there too, yes?'

Cal nodded and bit his bottom lip. And then he told them. He told them where his brother could be found.

'Good. I think you'd better give me your keys. Now about those drugs. Perhaps, Ste, you could fix Cal up now?'

And Ste did. He performed the task like a badly operated marionette. He cooked up a healthy dose, perhaps even an overdose, but enough anyway to send Cal up high enough not to feel too much of what came next.

Cal wept quietly and proffered his arm when Ste came at him with the needle. Cal looked at Ste, who was mostly not there at all, but just round the edges, in the corner of his eyes, Cal could sense Ste shrieking to be free. But to no avail. Once Ste had finished his task he fell back into his chair.

Danny and Peter didn't hesitate then. Danny leapt across the room at Ste, tore a hole in his neck and fed. Ste didn't resist. Peter went to his mother and did the same. She actually held her son as he drank her life away.

When Peter was done, he laid a small kiss on her cheek. Planted a rose.

Cal watched this as he drifted away on his cloud. He watched it and thought it terrible but didn't much care. He was starting to feel OK again. It had been a rough day. A crazy day. But now, now it was time to put all that behind him, time to forget about it all.

He was barely aware of them rattling around in the kitchen, and didn't feel a thing when Danny started sawing at his wrists with the serrated bread-knife.

He was already dead, his blood pooling across the floor at his feet, by the time they took his teeth.

5

The towers looked down on the feral scuttling form of the mother as she dragged herself home. She was in her early thirties and had been a mother longer than she had ever been just a girl. And she'd been on her own all along. Something she had inherited from her own mother. And *her* mother before that. A true child of the city. Born and bred.

She pulled her synthetic, zipped and hooded top tight round her frail and malnourished body against the cold. She didn't really feel the cold, her huddle against it muscle memory more than anything. The chemicals coursing through her veins in ever-diminishing amounts as she metabolised them, shielding her for now from the elements.

The key turned in the lock but the door resisted. Something snarled up on the floor on the other side. She pushed against it, squeezed into the flat and pulled one of the boys' coats up off the mat. She cursed and dumped it on the pile of coats and shoes avalanched against the wall just inside the door before closing it behind her. The coat rolled off the top of the pile back onto the mat, and lay in wait for whoever came in next.

The place was quiet. Deserted. She flicked on the light in the hall. Bedroom doors all shut. Kitchen, bathroom and living room doors all open onto darkened, silent rooms. She bashed on the first bedroom door. 'Cal. Cal, you in there? Cal!'

Bangbangbang.

Silence.

She turned the handle, pushed open the door and looked in. No one there.

By the light spilling in from the hallway she can see the glint of his discarded needle. She swore under her breath again and pushed the door further open, hit the light switch and headed in. He's not just left his needle lying there, he's left his little baggy of gear.

Silly boy.

She reached down, picked it up and pocketed it with a mean smile. 'Confiscated,' she chuckled to herself. Then she pushed herself upright, headed back out, pulling the door closed behind her, and headed across to the next bedroom door. She tapped gently on this door. 'Johnny? Johnny baby? You in there?' She put her ear to the door. Silence. She thought about going in and checking, but there was a little baggy of gear burning a hole in her pocket, so she decided to leave it for now. If he wasn't there it'd only fuck her off and there was nothing she could do about it, so why bother? He'd come back in the end. They always did.

Into her room next. It was immaculately tidy in here. Dirty though – hadn't ever been vacuumed or dusted, but everything was put away, and the bed made. Just in case. She reached under her bed and pulled out a small wooden cigar box. Her kit box.

Then across to the kitchen. Turned the cold tap on and poured herself a glass of water. Her mouth was gacky. She didn't rattle through the cupboards looking for food. She wasn't hungry. Tended not to be. And didn't really get food in. What's the point? Might as well eat out and then you didn't have to wash up. Bread, milk and jam generally covered it. One of the boys had been at the bread and jam. Left it out. Figures.

She headed on into the sitting room, dropped the cigar box onto the coffee table and fumbled her way across to the floor lamp on the other side of the room. She couldn't face the glare of the ceiling light. The lamp would give her enough illumination by which to sort herself out. Click. On. The curtains were closed. She turned back to the table and the tatty old seats positioned round it and screamed.

Sitting on the sofa facing the window, their backs to the door, were two children. One of them, a small black boy with strikingly pale eyes in his school uniform, a dark stain on one leg, and the other a white boy, baby, couldn't be even two yet, head shaved, wearing a wedding suit. They sat there and looked at her like two cats eyeing a mouse.

'What the fuck you doing here? Get out! Go on, fuck off! The pair of ya.'

Shrill.

'I am waiting for John to come home. He has something of mine,' both children said in unison. 'You can wait with me if you'd like.'

The children were bad. Not bad like John and Cal were bad – *they* were just little shits. These two were *wrong*. And they scared her – whatever weaknesses she may have, her instinct wasn't one of them. She stood and looked at them for a moment. They sat and stared unblinkingly back at her. She started to fidget and tried to think of a way of just removing herself from this situation. She couldn't understand why she was so terrified. But she was. Perhaps partly the drugs. Just sketching out. But it was definitely *them*, too. It wasn't just in her head. It was the way they talked. The way they said 'I' like there was just one of them. And the way they didn't blink, didn't move. And didn't seem to breathe.

'What's he got of yours?'

'A knife.'

She looked around the room then from discarded flotsam to abandoned jetsam, searching desperately for a knife, any knife, that she could give them to make them go away.

'It's not here, rat. I've already looked.'

That brought her eyes back to the staring little horrors on the sofa. The little one had ruby lips, like he'd been playing with his mother's lipstick. She pulled her gaze away from them and her eyes locked on to her cigar box on the table.

'Go on, rat. Take your filth and settle yourself down. I can only assume you don't know where he is?'

She shook her head, reached shamelessly for the cigar box, dropped onto the end of the other sofa furthest from the intruders and slid the wooden lid out on its groove. She made a concerted effort not to look at them as she prepared her medicine.

'You know, I sit here and I look at you, and I almost feel sorry for them. The boys, I mean. How else could they be?' the children pondered aloud. She felt their eyes on her. Her hands trembled, ever so slightly. She needed them steady for the next part. 'But then, by the same token, how far do we let things go before we say enough?' She stuck the needle into her arm and plunged.

She pulled the needle out and dropped it back, unclean, into the cigar box. The older child tilted his head, hopped down from the sofa and started to approach her. Now it was just he that spoke to her. 'You know what your children have done, don't you? The older one, Cal, he stabbed me as I sat on a park bench. Minding my own business. Waiting for the sun. He stabbed me because I wouldn't give him what he wanted. I didn't have what he wanted. But he stabbed me anyway.'

Her eyes were half-dopey now, and she half-listened. She looked at the child as he stood over her, telling her his story. The child then clambered up onto the seat next to her and continued with his tale. 'Now the younger one, John, he stabbed this child here, his leg.' The boy pointed to the stain-surrounded hole in his school trousers. 'I don't think he meant to. I think he was scared, and that perhaps he thought I was someone else, and what he did, he did defensively. But that doesn't change the fact that he left the boy to bleed on the floor and laughed when he went on his way. So you tell me: should I be expected to forgive them?'

She shook her head at that and mumbled in their defence. 'They're not bad kids, y'know? It's just their father left and it's been…'

The baby boy with the shaved head gazed at her dispassionately and licked his lips.

'Shhh, rat, shhh…' continued Danny, 'You are just saying words because you think that's what is supposed to be done. I'm sure their father never left. I don't doubt that he was never here in the first place. I'm sure he was just like them. Running around the rubble rutting with any bitch-rat that would open her legs. Isn't that so?'

'No,' she insisted. 'No. He was around and he left. He used to hit me. And Cal. Johnny was too little. He was gone before he was big enough to need hitting.'

Danny looked at her, considered her and decided to believe her.

'Oh. Well, good for you. Good for you! Perhaps then I can forgive *you*. But your boys: should I forgive them? For murdering me? Twice?'

'But they can't have murdered you… you're not dead…'

'Dead is relative, my dear sweet creature. Very relative indeed. Strangely enough, your boy Cal murdered me and I actually feel more alive than I have done in years. Many, many years. Sadly my plan was for the opposite. And so by giving me life, he has in fact taken it away from me: what is life without the freedom to choose what one does with it? Huh? Even if that choice is death? So he *has* murdered me. By taking my death, he has taken my life. And he's dumped it in darling little Peter here, and then put it in the hands of your John, who as we speak is running around this hell sticking me into anyone who happens into his path…' Danny turned and looked into her confounded face then, and a dark intent clouded his features: '…and it simply will not do. I need the knife, rat. Do you understand me?'

She nodded weakly. She didn't. Understand. At all. But she believed that he needed the knife.

'I have already dealt with Cal. He sent me here. I didn't forgive him.'

Danny reached across and put a small tissue-wrapped bundle in her lap.

'If you help me then I might forgive you. And I might forgive John. Although neither of you deserve it. What Cal did was unforgivable, and he has paid the price you will pay if you let me down.'

Danny nodded towards the bundle and she looked down at it, then back at Danny, then back at the bundle. Shaking, she reached her nervous fingers down and opened it out. At first she didn't understand what she was looking at. She thought it was outsized sweetcorn. Broken nuts, maybe.

'His teeth, rat. Cal's teeth.'

Danny pushed himself up from the sofa and went back to sit with Peter. The two children resumed their feline observance of the mother who, in spite of the tide of narcotics washing over her, now started to sob, silently, her bottom lip curled, rocking back and forth.

'Hush, rat. Hush. Remember what needs doing. Get me the knife. Or there will be no mercy.'

CHAPTER FIVE

OBSERVATION AND RENDITION

1

I left him a note and told him where I planned to do it. The bench. There could be no doubt. It was what he wanted, but I knew that he'd never admit it. I knew he'd never leave unless I left first. That he'd need someone to blame. Because that's how he was. How he is. How he has been for longer than I care to remember. He wasn't always this way.

Age does things. It makes one stubborn. And bitter. Gods, *so bitter.*

I remember when we were young. I remember how we would laugh, and fight, and make love. How we lived, with each other, by each other, for, in, of – pick a preposition and in all likelihood our lives at some points entwined as described. We thought it was love. And perhaps it was.

Perhaps it was.

I don't really know what love is, and I've spent much time considering it. As much time as anyone has considered anything. More, in fact. More even than him.

Because I am older than him. Much older. But he has long since lost that truth to the mists, as he has lost so many other truths. His perspective has clouded over and become unbearably opaque. For him, and by extension for me. He expects me to share his bitterness. He thinks it is absolute. Age does that too.

Yet he was *so* dear to me at the beginning, so *romantic*. Not in the sense of the word now. Back then it was something different. Back then the world was a different place. The nights were darker. Life was shorter. And these human creatures lived closer to nature. Their dreams were primitive reels of chasing across plains bearing weapons of stick and flint. But his dreams seemed different. His dreams were *more*. They were impossible, and they marked him out. He was full of lust and fury. He was glorious.

And he tasted so unlike anything else I'd ever tasted, I chose to keep him. He was my first of the new kind. More came after him. But he was my first, and that set him apart. I will accept my responsibility on that score: it was I who put him on the pedestal that eventually soured him.

For so long, he ran with me, hunted with me, lived with me, and he was beautiful.

But if beauty is in the eye of the beholder, then time serves only to blind us. Or perhaps time merely serves to erode beauty's myopia and reveal the base offal at our core, that writhing, desperate need to be something more than life-struck mud and barely repressible appetites. Engines of procreation and decay. Bubbling and gurgling towers of digestion and waste.

I don't know. I think these things, and I sound like him. I see him now, as he sees everything. That too, I suppose, has been gifted to us both by age.

After all these years, *lifetimes* really, I still don't even know what beauty is, much less love. Other than that once I found him beautiful, and that I remember thinking I loved him. But he changed. Of course he changed. Everything changed, everything changes. And perhaps that's what really happened to him – he *stopped* changing, stopped moving. And like a shark that stops swimming, the stasis brought him low. His vision clouded over and he lost sight of beauty. He started to hate. He started to die.

He got old.

And he expected me to get old with him.

But I couldn't do it. Because I wasn't like him.

When I tasted him that first time, when I gave him the gift, I did so unconditionally. I made no demands. No insistence that he be like me. And I didn't haunt him. Not as he chose to haunt others he passed the gift on to. He became *as* me, but he didn't *become* me. I didn't *become* him. The union of congress, for me, was to taste unity, oneness, and then to let go knowing there was another. That I wasn't alone.

It wasn't like that for him. He would never let go.

So he was my first, of the new kind, but he was a transgression and I have lived to regret him. I have lived and I have learnt. I am older and wiser. If I were to start again, I would do things differently.

I *have* started again.

It's not been easy. It has required a lot of planning.

Years in fact.

Money wasn't a problem – plenty of that squirrelled away over the centuries.

Nonetheless every step had to be taken slowly. Carefully. Because I knew he'd destroy me if he knew. That he'd tear my throat out in a flash if he so much as imagined my intent. Because he'd come to lean on me. He'd never let me go. He'd see me rise before he'd ever let me leave. And so I realised I had to make that lie a truth in his mind: I had to rise if ever I wanted to leave.

First I had to learn how to lie. And lying is not easy when there is no one else in the world like you. When you are the last of a long-extinct species. I wondered if I could have just run. But I would have had to run for ever. And he would never have stopped chasing me. And his hate would have mushroomed into something I daren't even consider. Something I need now to be careful to avert.

No. I had to convince him I'd gone.

And so first I had to find somewhere to hide.

I found this new one after some searching, and a number of false starts.

I had no interest in doing this his way. I would not invade, destroy and possess the way he does. The casual annexing of others as if they had no worth.

Because they are worth more than anything.

Everything.

Because the end of a consciousness is death; and death is

the end of all consciousness. There's no comeback, there's no going to heaven, that's it. There is no afterlife. Of that I am certain. There is nothing outside of the universe. Nothing beyond this existence. There is much more to this existence than might perhaps be apparent. But it is all contained within it. I should know. And so what he does, the way he does it, it is murder. It is the act of total destruction. It is absolute.

Feeding is one thing. There are ways and means. But it *is* possible to be decent.

I have regrets. Of course I do. I have done things I wish I hadn't. But I have chosen not to continue doing them. He has chosen to retreat into hate, from where he can justify what he does, the things he has done. They are rats. And it's nothing more than they deserve. He blames the victims of his sins for the sins he has perpetrated against them. Which is about as emblematic of their lower nature as anything I can think of. So his hatred of them is really his hatred of himself. Is it not always the case?

He fell into his hatred like a fever from which he never awoke, and into which he tried to drag me. He went *bad*. His habits macadamised, and he became a living fossil of something vicious and mindless. Everything he hated in them he embodied in himself. He would never change.

So I searched for a shell. One that I could inhabit without having to eviscerate. Because, unlike when I gave him the gift, this time I would have to inhabit this new one. I didn't know if it was possible. I was scared. What if it wasn't possible? What if there was no way it could be done? Well, if that was the case then perhaps I wouldn't fake it, perhaps I would stare into the sun and leave. Just as I'd started threatening to do.

I had to study their physiology. The science of the bodies they lived in. I needed a body that had been deserted. Boarded up. But which still functioned. That would stand up and walk away when I needed it to.

I searched in hospitals and eventually found a place where they lined them up in rows. They cared for them as much as one might expect given the circumstances of their condition. Their persistent vegetative states. They fed food and liquid into them through pipes, and allowed waste out through pipes too. And every day a physiotherapist would move from bed to bed to put them through basic motions that stopped them wasting away and curling into desiccated claws beneath their white blankets.

It took time to find the place.

It took time to figure out how to get in there.

And then I had to work my way through them until I found one that functioned.

I went through three of them before I found this one.

Those three all malfunctioned in one critical way or another. In the first, the left side of his body would only flail randomly in response to any given instruction. I gently stopped his heart.

The second was haunted by the ghost of its former occupier. I found her, wandering the halls of her broken mind with a candle, looking for the switch that would get things working again. I searched with her for a while. But every fuse box we found was blown beyond repair. I held her in my arms at the end, and shushed her. She cried. She didn't want to go. But nor did she want to stay. Not in the darkened sarcophagus within which she'd already spent far too long trapped. I held her, and quieted her. I stopped her heart too.

The third simply suffered massive organ failure within hours of me moving in.

But the fourth was deserted, I made sure. And everything worked. He had something of a limp, and a dramatic scar that ran from the tip of his cheekbone diagonally back across his temple and into his hairline. But he was young, and in good condition, and he *worked*.

All of this also had to be carried out in midwinter. Sunlight was always going to be a problem, but in the winter the likelihood of full, direct sunlight was always reduced. The sun might swing lower in the sky but it was further away, and that eased the intensity of its heat a little. That, coupled with more plentiful overcast days and perhaps a north-facing ward, and we might be getting somewhere. But nonetheless, blistering skin would attract attention. All of these things needed thinking about.

So the fourth one was good. He was weak. But, with my help, I got him out. And I got him back here. And I started to prepare him. Worked him out. Fed him. Made him strong. Made him *me*.

I made some reconstructive changes to his face – just enough to make him not him any more. I kept the scar though. Scars are sacred. And I took his name: Rider, James G.

Then I start making provisions. I prepared a home. I wanted to be free, but I had no intention of being alone.

I intended to give the gift to those who needed it, but not like I'd given it that first time, to the old-one. Not naïvely. I would give it responsibly this time. Things would be different.

I found help.

It all took time.

But if there's one thing I've got plenty of experience of, it's time.

Time is everything.

And eventually I was ready. All of this behind his back: the new body, the new home, family, all of it without him knowing. Until at last I was ready. I, the old, original I, wrote him the note and went to the bench. I waited for the sun. I waited for the sun, and I crossed my fingers.

I crossed my fingers and I smiled.

And I woke up as a man.

And he, *he*, had no idea.

He bought it, and he moped, and he burnt, and everything went according to plan.

Except for the knife.

The damned knife.

2

I track him through the park from a distance and watch as he takes his place on the bench. A CCTV camera blankly observes me trundle down the path. He sits there, upright, proud, reading the story of last week's burning in the newspaper in the orange glow of the street lamp that bathes the bench in light.

So, he has lasted a week. I'm not sure whether I am surprised or not. I wasn't convinced he'd do it. But it is more than a relief that he has chosen to put an end to things. I have built everything on the belief that he would.

It is cold. It always is. But he exhales no clouds as he breathes – because he doesn't breathe. He hasn't breathed for a very, very long time.

I tug the scarves tight round my mouth and chin, pull my coat's huge hood down low over my face, tuck my gloved hands into my pockets and wait in the darkness to make sure he goes, that he sees it through. I need to see it to believe it.

It is something of a surprise that he doesn't see me. Or smell me. I can smell him. Even from this distance. And I can see every wrinkle of his face, every crease of his coat. But he is sitting in the light. And I probably don't smell like I used to.

But still, he must be distracted.

A good sign.

Which is when the child enters the scene, stage right. He looks skittish from the off. I catch sight of his orange-outlined figure the moment he hoves into view from behind the stand of trees that the path curves round as it weaves its way out of the park and back towards the city. He is moving at something between a fast walk and a slow jog.

The sky is starting to brighten now. The shadows of the trees behind me starting to thicken across the ground before me like claws reaching across the field towards the old-one on the bench.

The child stops at the bench and the old-one looks up at him.

This could complicate matters.

But hopefully not so much that I will need to alter any plans.

The child, hopping from foot to foot, pulls something from his pocket, a blade surely, and the old-one smiles at him. That old, hateful smile. And I know then that the child will come to harm. But there is nothing I can do about that. We all come to harm one way or another, and it is our own responsibility to avoid and to recover from. We can't all be saved.

Then things happen quickly.

The old man says something to the child, who then slaps the old-one. The old-one catches the child in a flash and the child squeals, his arm caught, and in all likelihood snapped. More fool him. The child, almost in a reflex action, thrusts his blade into the old-one's side. That's when the sun breaches the treeline behind me and the burning starts.

At which point I begin to relax. It is pretty much done. I start to move away, down the path on this side of the park, back towards the safe house. I watch the end of it across my shoulder as I start away.

Then something happens that stops me in my tracks.

The child pulls himself, and his knife, free. And the knife is glowing. But the glow is more than hot. It is alive. Festering. And it speaks to me. It speaks nonsense, the babble of one lost in the deepest sleep. It tells me that we might not be done. The child, in his hood, carrying his broken arm, stuffs the still-glowing blade in his pocket and pelts from the park. I pause, unsure, uncertain that what I *felt* wasn't just a refusal to accept that it was done. That my mind hadn't constructed a madness to prolong the nightmare of his continued existence. But uncertainty will not do. I have to be certain. I've waited too long to leave anything to chance.

So I give chase. I am faster than the child. And I know how to track.

The next camera I pass is too slow to catch me. I am motion-blur, at best.

I follow him down into the tunnels and maintain my distance. He's not paying any attention anyway – he's in too much pain. A guard at the gate straightens up when he sees me approach the barriers, but when I pull out a travelcard and wave myself through he quickly loses interest. No law against tramps down here. Just tramps without tickets.

We head a few stops north and then up and out. The sun is up, but it hangs low in an overcast sky. And of course I came prepared. My hood, my coat. Scarves. Gloves. The perfect disguise. Everyone looks the other way.

The boy heads deeper into the concrete underbelly of the estates, in between the towers, and I follow him. Through, up, along until he reaches his destination. I linger in a stairwell and listen to him bashing on a door down the way.

'Ste mate, you there? Open up, mate…'

A brief pause.

'It's me mate, it's Cal. Lemme in, yeah?'

Another pause. He doesn't seem too welcome.

'What do you think I fucking want Ste. You want me to make an announcement or what? Open the door man.'

Only then is the door unlatched and opened.

'You're not letting the twat in are you Ste? I thought I told you to tell him to…' A screech from further back, from somewhere in the bowels of the flat that has just opened up to the boy.

'Donnashutup! It's not like… Jesus Christ Cal… what happened your arm?'

'Don't ask. You got any?'

'Course I got some. But what happened your arm?'

'I said don't ask, didn't I? Fuck's sake, man, just sort me out…'

Then the door closes and he's in and I have a moment to think. I edge down the gantry, listening closely to each door as I pass, listening for the sound of him. I don't have to lean in to the doors, I just focus my ears. My hearing is as sharp as my vision. Which helps. Some of the flats are silent. It's not that early, but nor is it yet get-up-and-go time. Not for this lot. A few rustles and bumps of activity from behind some of the doors – breakfasts being prepared, early-morning TV. The door behind which the boy has disappeared offers the muffled sounds of televised rutting, and of them talking. The smell of dog-shit and drug sweat. A bad place. One of many.

And then a child screams, and the volume of it nearly splits my head. They have a child in there with them. A baby.

Oh god.

I lean in to the door and put my eye to the keyhole and I see the boy fall back and drop the knife to the floor, and in that instant I *know*. I just know it. I step back from the door and towards the stairwell, my mind in turmoil.

He is still alive. And he is in the knife.

And soon enough he will awaken in the child.

And what then?

The old fear reawakens within me, the fear of *him*. A small, bold, reckless part of me urges me to break down the door and rip out all their throats, bleed the baby, the poor baby, take the knife and be done with him, once and for all. The rest of me dares not: too many variables.

He may already be in one of the others.

I've spent too long hiding everything from him to blow it now, this close to him being gone. I scuttle back down the stairwell and across the square at the bottom, and find myself a covered corner opposite where I can sit and wait before deciding what to do next.

And I fret.

A few hours later the boy comes back down and makes his way along the front of the tower before cutting across the square, across towards me. I examine his posture, the hang of his coat: does he have it on him? Or did he leave it behind? The awkwardness of his posture because of his arm, and his desire not to look any more suspicious than absolutely necessary, make it hard to tell. But as he comes closer to me, it becomes obvious that there is something weighty in one of his coat pockets. I have to assume it is the knife. And I have to decide now: stay with the child, the infected baby, or follow the knife.

I look back up at the flat and make an assessment: the child won't be going anywhere. Not immediately. The old-one will want to control the baby. He wanted to burn. He won't allow the baby to infect anyone else. Assuming, once again *assuming*, that it works like it usually does and that control is an option.

Fuck! What a mess. Fuck.

The knife, on the other hand, he has no control over. The knife is the key variable in this disastrous equation so, for now, better to follow the boy, to stay with the knife.

The boy heads two blocks over and then up and in.

So I now have the old-one grid-referenced. He is in two places.

Time to find somewhere from which I can watch, and wait, and remain undiscovered.

Time to sit back and see how this plays out.

Damn him.

Damn him to hell.

I smile at that.

Knowing him like I do, hell is exactly what this will be for him.

It would be poetic if it wasn't such an egregious catastrophe.

Fuck.

Back into the shadows.

Again.

3

Like moths to a flame they come from all around. The blue flashing lights and the police tape all but irresistible. They come and they watch and they listen and learn and almost by osmosis they start to know what has happened. Murder. Kidnap. Ritualised. Underworld.

A lot of them know of them. If they've not scored off them themselves, then they've known people who have. A lot of the folk in the crowd are perfectly upstanding and suitably appalled. These people have made their beds, they think, and now they are lying in them. They are appalled. But they are not surprised. They pity the children. Everyone pities the children.

Even the children.

John and Bobby sit on a wall at the back of the crowd and look up towards the fourth floor, where the police arc lights throw a glow. They sit with a small group of younger people, most of them a bit older than themselves, maybe one or two ever so slightly younger, and they all compare notes.

It's definitely Ste and Donna. Ste was a cunt. Donna was a slag. Is the baby dead? Who knows – the baby's gone. Serious? That's what I heard. There was some other poor fuck in there too. Hands chopped off. Hands chopped off?! Hands chopped off and put in a fire. Fuck off. Nah man, I know the guy that found 'em. He lives in one of the flats next door, innit? He went in to put the fire out, found the poor fucker's hands. All puffed up and shit like baked potatoes. Laughter.

What about the dog? Who gives a fuck about the dog? Just askin'? Dog's dead too.

Fuckin' hell.

Cool.

Bobby ducks into one of the flats behind them with one of the older kids to skin up, and they get a bit stoned. Another of the older kids has skinned up too. So they sit there smoking and shooting the shit and they get to talking about their day. And they get braggy. John doesn't mention stabbing a little kid. He's not sure people would be too impressed. But he reckons that they'd be impressed his brother knew them. The dead guys in the flat. And some of them are. Impressed that is. And some of them joke that maybe it was John's brother with his hands cut off. They call him stumpy. They all laugh.

John doesn't laugh.

John doesn't laugh because someone was after his brother this afternoon.

They'd chased him down the street. Ricky and his crew.

And isn't that them? Over there, down by the police tape? John's eyebrows furrow and he sits up straighter and he watches like a hawk. He can't see Ricky, but the rest of them fit the bill. He pulls the knife out of his pocket and slides the blade out a single notch. Just in case. It's one of the younger kids that notices it.

'Whatcha got?'

John ignores him. Doesn't even hear him. He's too busy keeping watch on the threat down by the tape. The younger child reaches out to investigate, touches it and pulls his finger back with a sharp hiss. He yowls and tears spring into his eyes. John doesn't notice. Most of them don't notice. But one of them does. This one slightly older.

'What the fuck you got there Johnny?'

John notices *this* lad. He has to. John is junior to this one, and one must respect one's seniors. Them's the rules. He glances his way, keen not to lose track of the guy from earlier. 'What? This? It's just a knife innit?'

The other kids start tuning into the conversation then, one by one. These little moths have found a new little flame. The younger child who has nicked himself is making quite the silent fuss, hopping from foot to foot, alternately sucking and then shaking his finger.

'Let's have a look,' says one of them, reaching for it.

John pulls it away. 'No man, fuck off. It's mine.' His eyes still flitting down towards the tape and the group of older, meaner youths over there. The senior pack. On patrol.

The younger pack start getting a bit jostly then. They want to see the knife. Another one makes a half-hearted snatch for it. John thrusts one shoulder forward and swings the knife instinctively away, but another child, a girl, is coming in from the other side. It snicks across the back of her hand. She leaps back with a scream as if burnt. Heads turn their way.

All of the younger children take a step back then and look at John. The girl is making a right old song and dance. Some of the bystanders beyond this little huddle start peering into the circle and they see the knife. It glints. They start commenting, quietly at first, but with increasing volume. The kids themselves get their backs up and start snapping and snarling at John. What the fuck you doing? Why'd you cut her? She ain't done nothing.

They form a pack and start to close in.

John, his back against the wall, feels the terror well up within him. He's seen this too many times before. But before, he'd always been one of the others, part of the larger group, closing in.

And down the front, the senior pack prick up their ears. They smell blood. They start in towards this new entertainment. John, senses in a heightened state of alert once more, sees one of them gesturing across the mob to someone else. John looks desperately round, certain that he'll see Ricky bearing down on him.

He sees him too late. Ricky pushes through the loose perimeter of John's acquaintances, his toothy smile underscoring the gimlet darkness in his eyes. John bites his lip, hesitates for the briefest of moments, before swooning into the arms of panic. He screams and starts swinging the knife.

Ricky leaps back with a hiss.

John snicks two more children. Three.

They howl.

The immediate huddle fall back and the broader crowd then start to low and moo and wash back and forth.

John drops his head then and runs at them, pushing his way through, flailing. He has no idea if anyone else gets nicked by the knife, he doesn't care because he's out then and he's breaking for home.

He doesn't stop running, he doesn't look back.

4

The sound of the herd back at the scene chases him for a block or two, but the greater gravitational pull of the triple murder soon pulls them back into their tight orbit of morbid curiosity. As he nears home John slows and eventually does take a glance over his shoulder. How many times in one day can this keep happening? He has escaped them. Again. He is on his own. Again. He drops his head, turns and trudges the final furlong.

At the foot of his block he looks up towards the flat. No lights on in the larger window beside the front door. Cal is out. Or still out for the count. Out of the way, either way.

At least there's that.

The smaller window of the door is aglow though, and that means his mother is still up. Although she's always up. Doesn't mean she's conscious. He would in fact be very surprised if she was. He hopes he'll be able to sneak in without disturbing her. She'd just get on his case and he isn't in the mood.

He heads for the stairwell that leads up to his floor. A shadow is waiting there for him. He freezes. The shadow stands and moves towards him. The knife is out of his pocket without a moment's hesitation and is held up in front of him.

The shadow raises its hands in a calming gesture and says, 'Child.'

John stops backing away, but remains very much on his guard. 'What you want?'

'You are in danger, child. If you go up there, you will probably die. Like your brother.'

'What the fuck you talking about?' The sound of broken glass in his voice. He is at his limit now. Not much more he can take. 'How'd you know who my brother is?'

'Because I have been watching. And you are in danger. Your brother has got himself into some trouble hasn't he?'

Images of bigger kids chasing him down the street. He nods. 'Maybe. What of it?'

'Your brother has got *you* into trouble, hasn't he?'

John wilts somewhat then, and the tears come. He is tired and scared and alone. And this shadow *knows*. And *no one* is supposed to know. He lowers the knife and the shadow takes another step closer.

'Well, the trouble is up there, child. It is waiting for you. And if you go up there, it will kill you like it killed the others. It won't hesitate. It will show no mercy.'

'The others? You mean…?' Images then of blue lights and police tape. Burnt hands. Stumpy. His head a swirl of confusion and conflict. The day has been more than the usual amalgam of bedlam and strife, but he hasn't given it any weight.

'Your brother is dead, child, and you will be too if you don't trust me and come with me now.'

The shadow takes another step towards him. John glances back up to the flat. The door opens and someone comes out. John steps instinctively into the shadows and watches as his mother steps across to the balcony and looks down. She scans all around, looking for something. Or someone.

Looking for him.

She never looks for him.

He takes a sharp intake of breath and in that instant believes every word the shadow has spoken. He nods, 'OK.'

Then the shadow takes his hand and leads him away. And the shadow now knows what it had suspected since the dawning of the light this morning. It knows that the knife carries the trace of the old-one. It knows that the nightmare is not yet over. Or perhaps that it is over, and that a new one has begun.

But the child from the tower has taken its hand and departed, away from the towers and the troubles that lie among them.

CHAPTER SIX

PESTILENCE AND PAIN

1

It was the home of The Original Gutbuster™. It was open twenty-four hours a day. The food was greasy, the coffee brutal. And it was where Tom and Anna retreated shortly after midnight to try and gather their thoughts.

None of it made any sense, and it was getting even less logical with every new development. And it wasn't that they weren't making any connections either. It's that they were making too many.

Anna took a seat in one of the booths beneath the mirror that ran the full length of the wood-panelled diner. The lights were too bright. Left nothing to imagination. Right now, that was a distinct plus as their imaginations were running away from them. Tom went to the counter to fetch coffee. And he tried to focus.

Anna seemed to be coming apart at the seams. Which was fine. The slaughter at the flat was distressing. No two ways about it. But she was acting strange now. Tom knew they had their differences existentially, and worried that her propensity to assume the worst perhaps meant she had nowhere to go in the face of this, philosophically speaking, to hold it together. He didn't know for sure. She was a pretty closed book. All he knew was that she was fraying at the edges. And that he hadn't seen that coming. But then he hadn't seen any of this coming. How could he have?

He was handed two cups of coffee without a smile. He paid for them and took them across to the booth. Anna sat with her head forward over the table, roughly rubbing her eyes with the thumb and forefinger of one hand while her other hand rested on the table in front of her.

'Here.'

She looked at her coffee, then up at Tom, and smiled weakly. Her eyes were bloodshot, exhausted-looking. She winced against the bright lights of the diner.

'How you feeling?'

She shrugged and sighed and held on to her coffee. She didn't drink any. 'Head hurts,' was all she offered. Tom nodded, raised his coffee to his lips and blew across the surface to cool it before taking a sip.

'Alright. Look. How sure are you that it was him?' Tom asked her.

'One hundred percent.'

News of Danny's body going AWOL from the hospital had reached them at the flat. And initially it was just another bunch of shit that had happened today in the city. Until Anna had asked to see what the boy had looked like. They'd shown her. And then she'd called Tom to one side and had told him, 'I saw him earlier. Going down the stairs. He had a little boy with him.'

'You saw who?'

'Danny.'

Tom hadn't been able to digest that. 'But… you were with me at the block earlier?' Tom had assumed she must have come to the estate sometime during the day, if she thought she'd seen him. But couldn't figure out why.

'No. He was coming down the stairs when we were heading up. I saw him.'

'You mean just now?'

'Yeah. Well. Hour or two ago. How long have we been here?'

'It can't have been him. He was stabbed this afternoon. He would have been dead, Anna. It was probably just a kiddy that looked like him.'

'I'm telling you it was him,' she insisted, a troubled look in her eyes.

Tom had taken a deep breath when she'd first taken him to one side and told him, and he took another one now, in the diner. 'How can you be so sure?'

'Because I just *know*,' she insisted, that strange, conflicted look in her eyes again. Intense. Slightly loopy. But utterly insistent.

Tom leant back against the leatherette banquette and held her gaze. She didn't blink. In the end he did. He put his hands up and said, 'OK. OK. So it was him. Which means that…' he laughed tiredly, '… fuck knows what it means.'

What it meant was that *everything* might be connected, and if that was the case then it all started just over a week ago, with someone burnt on a bench. No witnesses. Nothing on CCTV of any use. No body. Some ash and a few bones. No DNA matches. Nothing. That on its own would be weird enough. Even if it had been a suicide: how? How does a person make themselves burn from the inside out, leaving nothing? Or, assuming it was murder, how do you do that to someone? Fill them with petrol and… what? Make them swallow a lit cigarette? Even then it'd surely just explode, if that. They wouldn't keep burning once the petrol was burnt. And even if they did, the bench would burn too. So no. Essentially we're talking about textbook spontaneous human combustion here, but you can jog on if you thought Tom was going to put that in any report.

So that's one thing.

Then it happens again a week later. Same time, same place. Only this time we have at the very least a witness, and perhaps even a perpetrator. So maybe some answers. And the universe starts its inexorable spin back into alignment. Find the guy with the broken arm and find out what he saw. What he did.

Fine.

But by the time they find him he's been executed. Along with two junkies who've had their throats ripped out. And a dog that's been bitten to death by a small child. But the guy with the broken arm, he's not just dead, he's had his teeth and hands removed. They've since found the hands – burnt, in a box full of toys, also burnt, in the bedroom of the child of the murdered junkie female.

The small child is missing.

The hands and teeth thing Tom thinks he understands – no teeth, no hands: no ID. They'd found the hands in the burning box in the kid's room. Scorched. No fingerprints. The teeth hadn't been with them. Whoever it was that had carried out the atrocity in the flat, they didn't want the police to know who the boy with the broken arm was. Which, as far as Tom was concerned, meant that that's what they needed to know more than anything.

And then there was Danny.

Danny was nothing to do with any of the above. Not that Tom could see, anyhow. But here was Anna saying she saw him leading a little boy away from the flat. From which a little boy was missing. But this all takes place about five or six hours after Danny was stabbed and killed.

'Right. So the dead kid left the hospital, went to the flat, killed everyone and stole the baby,' Tom said, almost smiling. 'Case solved. Let's go home.' He took another slug of his coffee and tried really hard to think. Then he just fired questions at Anna.

'Why would they not want us to know who he is? Could the bench killings be assassinations? Like, I dunno, Russian secret service? That would explain how fucking weird they were. Maybe our guy with the arm saw something he shouldn't have and they followed him to the flat. Shut him up. Took the baby with them. No loose ends.' He shook his head. 'Christ, listen to me.'

Anna looked at him and didn't drink her coffee. 'I feel funny.'

Tom regarded her but didn't see or hear her. 'But you saw Danny with the baby. Except Danny died this afternoon. But then again, where's his body?' His eyes widened and his arm stopped with his coffee midway from the table to his lips. 'Tell me they've checked the CCTV at the hospital? They must have, surely?'

Anna shrugged.

'OK. So we've lost our witness or whatever to the burnings. So that's a dead end. We can't ID him, nothing. We've got nothing. Except you seeing Danny leaving with the baby. Which is fucking insane, because Danny is dead. But his body *is* missing. So… maybe the hospital fucked up. But there's no way Danny did all that in the flat…'

'Why not?'

That shook Tom from his join-the-dots reverie. 'Huh?'

'Why not?' Anna repeated.

'Why not what?'

'Why is there no way Danny did all that in the flat?'

Tom sneered at her then, his patience reached and beached at her relentless cynicism. 'Because he's fucking ten years old, Anna. On his own. How the fuck would a ten-year-old do that, to people like that, *on his own*. Jesus Christ.' He shook his head.

'You'd be surprised what children can do these days, Tom.'

He looked at her, and leant ever so slightly away from her. She seemed different. There was something in her eyes that he didn't like. Something unhinged. All of a sudden he wasn't sure that the words she was saying were anything more than the finest of veils thrown feebly in front of a seething mass of collapsing attachment to reality. She seemed as if the abyss was now well and truly looking into her. And that she knew it. Welcomed it, even.

He wasn't sure how to respond. And so he searched for something real, a logical avenue of investigation, anything that they could do that might work as a temporary tether to reconnect her to the real world. He wasn't sure she necessarily deserved his concern, but it was in his nature to try. 'Look, Anna… OK… I think what we need to do is find the person who stabbed Danny. We know that he was stabbed. It's the only fucking solid thing in all of this. So let's start there and see where it takes us. Yeah? Let's just forget all the rest of it, and find them.'

She looked at Tom then and smiled. It was a cold and terrible smile. 'I'll tell you who stabbed Danny, Tom. Children did it. Filthy little rat-children. You'll see. But you'll never understand. You're too soft.'

She pushed her untouched cup of coffee away and stood up. 'I feel funny,' she stated distractedly before getting up and wordlessly walking out of the diner.

Tom, his mouth agape, watched her go.

He would never see her again.

2

When they wake up, they wake up hungry.

The youngest one, the boy who first noticed the knife in John's hand the night before, he wakes up with a start just before dawn. He has had terrible dreams. Something has been plaguing him. It has been howling with frustrated rage and unbridled hatred, rattling around within him, shouting commands, but simultaneously tugged in other directions.

This boy, whose name is Liam, wakens with an ache in his belly, and a pain in his head that the burgeoning gloom at the window only seems to make worse. He closes the curtains. He has never closed the curtains before. He's ten. Why would he have? Not his job. But this morning he does. It's not enough. So he strips the sheet from his bed, clambers carefully up onto the top bunk (he doesn't want to wake his little sister), and stuffs the cloth over the top of the curtain rail. It'll have to do.

'Whatcha doing, Liam?' Megan mumbles sleepily.

He turns to her and tells her to go back to sleep. 'Just fixing the curtains Meg,' he says. He loves his sister more than anything. She's the best. Not that he'd tell anyone. Especially not her. But she knows.

She peeps suspiciously out from under her duvet, and only believes him once she sees the window. Then she rolls over on her side and pulls up the duvet and snuggles down.

Liam watches her do this, aghast and afraid. Because something inside him thinks of her as a rat. And that same part of him wants to bite her. To feed on her. He hurries back down from the top bunk and curls up on his own, pulls his knees in and shivers. He can't get back to sleep. His heart is whickering. The cut on his finger burning unbelievably. Something is wrong, he knows it.

Something is very wrong.

Three, perhaps four, streets across the city from where Liam is wedging his sheet into the top of the curtain rail, Leanne is woken by the sharpest pain in her abdomen that she's ever known. Worse than period pain. Way worse. It burns. And it sends tendrils up into her belly. These tendrils insinuate hunger, but the fire down below distracts her for now. Leanne's window has a blackout blind behind the curtain so she's not too worried about the coming of the sun.

There is a small, mean voice in her head ranting and raving, wailing and gnashing, but it is all too easy to ignore. The pain in her womb is just too much. She moans. And she curses Jamie's name – she'd told him to wear a condom, but he'd said it didn't matter if she was on the pill. They'd both been pissed. And a little bit stoned. They'd done it in the stairwell of the multi-storey car park after they'd left the crime scene last night. It wasn't even that good. He'd kept complaining about how the cut on his hand hurt. Didn't stop him wanting to do it though. Needs must.

And now he'd gone and given her something.

Arsehole.

A couple of stops away on the Underground, Jamie himself is still awake. He never got to sleep. He'd stayed up smoking spliff and drinking whisky, hoping that it would take the edge off the flaming agony of the gash across his palm. It didn't help. The last hour or so, the thought of anything other than meat turned his stomach. But the idea of meat, rare as you like, was almost more than he could bear. He thought about heading out, down to the convenience store and getting some, but the sky was brightening and the light was like needles in his eyes. He couldn't face it. The chatter in his head is a little livelier than he's used to, but only a little. He's long since learnt to tune it out. He does so again now.

He thinks he might have got tetanus or something from that knife.

When he catches up with that little John bastard he is going to wring his neck.

Back on the block now, within throwing distance of the flat that was the focus of so much attention the previous night, Amber is pacing the hallway. She can't get this voice out of her head. He is telling her to come to him, but she is scared. She doesn't feel right and her head is splitting. She goes to the front door, opens it quietly and looks out onto the balcony. The dawn is throwing shadows, but we've at least a half-hour's grace before the sun might break out of its cage. Amber looks out and doesn't know why she fears the coming of the light, just that she does fear it. Deeply.

But the voice in her head commands her: 'Move. Now, rat. Before it is too late. Come to me and you might make it through the day.'

She almost decides then to make a break for it. She almost cedes control to him, almost lets him take her and bring her to where he is waiting. Almost. But she doesn't quite trust him. She thinks he might be lying. He screams and thrashes at her impertinence. She retreats back into the gloom of her flat and hides from the sun.

3

Anna wanders the streets alone. She is confused and troubled. Her hand hurts. She has seen too much, gone through too much, and she feels like she is losing herself. The part of her that had always held hope at bay seems now to have grown teeth, and it is snarling and snapping.

She isn't sure what she said to Tom. It hadn't been her. She knows that words had come from her mouth, but she doesn't remember what they were, or where they had come from. This has never happened before. She wasn't weak. She'd never been weak. Pessimistic? Yes. Cynical? Arguably. But weak? No. Unprofessional? No.

Fucking mental? No.

She doesn't know what is happening to her, but something *is* happening to her. Something has got into her and it's trying to take control of her. And it might well be succeeding.

She holds the memory of Tom's face in her mind. His face when she spoke her last words to him in the diner. The face that said that he didn't know her. That she had lost it. And he had been right. She had lost it. She is still lost.

But now, as she walks down street-lit roads, past late-night kebab shops spilling out drunks and the desperate, she knows that she is lost. That something happened to her at the flat and it has catapulted her to somewhere she has never been before. Somewhere apart from her self. She felt like a ghost, haunting her own being. Like an echo trapped in the shell of the someone she used to be.

She allows her feet to transport her. Muscle memory, taking her home. She desperately tries to concentrate, to pull herself together. She feels a bit like she does when she's had far too much wine and crossed that line and has to walk and walk and walk until she's sobered up. She feels unmoored, unhinged, detached. All of these things. But different. Because she's hasn't touched a drop. She's stone-cold sober. And this doesn't make any sense.

'I feel funny,' she repeats, over and over under her breath. She doesn't attract any glances. She's not unusual. Not the first to have gone wrong around here.

Her hands are cold. She clenches them, unclenches them, gives them a shake. They won't warm up. She feels light-headed. Cold sweat. Her heart is skittery.

The scene at the flat had shaken her up. No doubt. You can't prepare yourself for that kind of thing. But being jaded helps. She hadn't expected it. But she'd known that one day it would happen. She'd had two not dissimilar days in her career. One was a murder-suicide. A father had decided time was up for his wife and two sons. He'd done that quietly, with a knife. In the night. No note. That had been five years ago now. The other had been human traffic, suffocated in the back of a lorry. Ukrainian. Mostly. A couple of Afghans in there too. That's what they figured. They'd looked Afghan. And that was as much identification as those two particular teenagers had enjoyed before they'd been cremated. The Ukrainians mostly had some paperwork on them. Got sent home – in boxes of course, but still… That lorry hadn't been good. They'd been looking for heroin. Hadn't found it. You win some…

Actually… you don't.

She pauses for breath and looks around and can't remember how she got here from the lorry. Then she remembers the lorry had been three years ago. Or was it four?

Where is she?

She needs to get home. She's not right. She keeps slipping away. Floating. Down here we all float. Where had she read that? Because she was floating now. Floating away, like a balloon blowing into the wind.

'Couldja spare a bit of change, love? Just need a couple of pounds to get the bus home.'

He teeters and totters and smells of cheap booze and after-thought. His fingers are puffed up and hardened. Claw-like. His shell-suit has a sweaty sheen.

She feels herself straighten. Her eyes narrow. And words bubble up in her throat, cruel, disgusted words that aren't hers. But with which she has a certain empathy. The verminous street specimen troubling her for money appals her, as this new part of her is vocalising. To his face. She would never have played her hand so aggressively. Wasn't her style. She was meek. Perhaps the flat had been a final straw, had unleashed her true, furious self. Perhaps now she would turn maniac.

She feels like a potentially murderous cliché from a cheap revenge film. But she doesn't kill him. She pushes past him and breaks into a trot.

'Come on love… just a bit of change…', his last-ditch plea before shouting after her, 'Well fuck off then, you bitch!'

Underground station just up ahead. She can get home if she just holds it together. Concentrates.

On the train, in the tunnels, it is quiet. Nearly last train. Everyone is detritus. As is she. She closes her eyes and floats. Her hands are getting colder. Her heart feels weak. Her wrist aches. Throbs. Insistently. She goes to the place where it hurts and she rides the pain. It keeps her steady. Ensconced in the darkness behind her eyelids the throb acts like a beacon, a dark star for her to orbit. A centre of gravity. A supermassive black hole.

She orbits and drifts back through this inner space to the flat. Past the child's room with the flames and the stink. She remembers the initial stab of sadness followed by the crash of the portcullis slamming down against her emotions. The child might not be here. Don't assume anything until you know. Hope someone else finds the body. Chalk it up when they do. Job done. Into the sitting room with the corpses and the blood.

She sighs.

She stops at the door and she takes it in. The mother on the sofa with the rose on her cheek. The man – the father? – in the chair with the hole in his throat. And the man, the *boy*, they'd been looking for, seated and facing her. His hands gone. His face destroyed.

His jaw hanging loose. Down and to the left. Like he was faking a laugh at a bad joke.

The train stops. She opens her eyes. One more stop until home. A short hop. She feels queasy. The lights too bright. And for a very brief moment she is fully back within herself. Fully here. She watches the cables lining the tunnels whip up and down and round each other in the light from the train, occasional sparks from the tracks throwing the brickwork into even sharper relief. At the next station she pushes herself up and out of her seat and almost blacks out. Her legs buckle and twang and she leans against the wall and fumbles her way up and out. Back into the streets. She drifts away again, back into space. And once again she is back in the flat.

Back in the room. Taking it all in. Dealing with it.

Three dead people.

And a dog, on the table.

And it's the dog that gets to her. The dumb, fucking animal.

That's when she gets the lump in her throat.

She moves into the room, across to the table, and looks down on the dog. He lies there, not breathing, his eyes full of sadness. And fear. He is covered in bite marks. She bets there are bruises beneath his pelt. She reaches down and gently touches his cheek with the back of her knuckles. Poor thing.

The dog snaps and snags a chunk out of her wrist.

One final reflex before death.

She snatches her hand back. She doesn't scream or cry out or make any sound at all. She is too shocked. Her heart in her throat. But that is the moment everything inside her starts to seep out. Her disgust. Her rage. Her abhorrence.

Her terror and her frailty.

She weighs anchor then and sets sail for where she is now. And where she is now is in the lift heading up to her flat. She needs to lie down. She is nearly there.

She goes into the flat, throws her coat on the chair in the hall. Then she goes from room to room closing the curtains. In the living room she stands at the window and looks out on the city. There is so much to see that nothing stands out. It looks like a dungheap littered with orange glow-worms. And it goes on and on and on. In the distance, glass cathedrals of commerce are hidden somewhere in the dark November night. She doesn't know why she stays here. She doesn't have anywhere better to go.

'You stay here because you are a rat, just like all the rest of them,' she intones meanly to her faint reflection in the glass before her.

Then she closes that final set of curtains, turns to the sofa and falls onto it. She cries a little bit then. And she thinks of her parents. She thinks of them and thinks that they were kind. That *they* weren't rats. But they were the only ones. That maybe he is right. He that is in here with her. Maybe he is right. And that maybe, at last, she's found someone who feels the same way she does. She closes her eyes. She stops breathing. And she sleeps.

She doesn't put any food down for the cat. She doesn't have a cat.

Never had.

And now she never will.

4

Ricky lives in a basement bedsit on his own, the only window a pavement-level frosted pane of glass affording the murkiest of illumination. He has spent the night listening to the voice in his head and has decided he can go fuck himself. He didn't invite him in and so he doesn't have to listen to him. But Ricky has an inkling. An inkling that he has become something else. And he welcomes the change. He pushes himself up from his bed and massages his belly. It is growling. It is hungry. The pain in his arm has retreated now – the fierce burn of it. He still can't believe that little John bastard knifed him. The child will pay for that. But not before Ricky has dealt with the snarling hunger in his gut.

He pads across the room to the front door, opens it and puts it on the latch. He peers into the darkened communal hallway beyond, his vision peculiarly acute. He peers, and he listens, and he pauses. He smells the air.

There are two more doors leading off the hallway. One of them houses those two miserable fat old cunts who are always bitching about his music. The other one a cute chick who moved in only a month or two back. She seems nervy, but hasn't given him any shit. Yet. Bit anorexic? Maybe. Issues? Very probably. Whatever.

His stomach growls again.

He makes his decision then, and steals silently across to her flat, his feet bare. He presses his ear against the door and listens. He can hear the TV murmuring in the space beyond.

He knocks quietly. A few moments later the door opens a crack and she peeps anxiously out.

'Hey, sorry. Any chance I could borrow a cup of sugar?'

'You serious?'

He smiles devilishly. 'Deadly.'

She actually laughs at that. Which is good, because if she hadn't he would have barged in and forced the issue. As it is she swings the door open and invites him in. He stays for a few hours, and he shares his new gift with her. And then, later on that same day, they head next door for lunch.

This is how it goes.

This is how a plague catches light and starts to smoulder across the yawning maw of the concrete-splintered city, hiding in the shadows from the extinguishing light of the sun.

And this is how the young seize power from the faltering hands of the old.

CHAPTER SEVEN

SUNBURN AND DEADLIGHT

1

He wasn't always like this.

There was a time, long ago now, when he was so alive. Not this living dead thing. Not this coiled serpent, spitting and snapping and raging. There was a time when I wasn't scared of him. When I didn't hate him. When he was beautiful. And good.

And I loved him. So much.

But watching the eruption of blood and carnage, borne on a wave of whispered terrors and misplaced blame – the usual: immigration, the poor, the blacks, the whites, the them, not us – that sweeps the towers, it's almost impossible to feel anything but hate, and I despair of it all.

Yet I know that despair is just as useless as hope. Both are simply costumed hesitation, and they are for the weak. But

I *do* hesitate. Am I now weak? Curse this fear that he has stewed over centuries into my marrow. I am free of him, and yet here he is, again, as always, destroying everything I see, everything I am.

Damn him.

I have all the cards. I have the boy. I have the knife. I have my anonymity – he doesn't even know I exist any longer! And yet I lurk and watch and I wait. And for what?

And so the first days and weeks blur by – *the caboose got loose, and smooshed the hoose…* I laugh at that. At least I still know how to be an idiot. I laugh again. It's not funny. Nothing is funny. Was it ever? Oh shut up… for god's sake…

At which point, belatedly, a moment of clarity in the orange-painted concrete shadows: go home. Rest. Think. Let it go. Come back at it from a different angle. There is no new information here. No murder here is significantly different to the thousands, millions of others that have been observed over the years. No sundered artery or mournful infant death rattle that hasn't played out in some variation or other before. No eventual outcome that will ever be final.

When did I become susceptible to all of these mortal assumptions? When did I forget that there is no destination, no purpose, nothing more than the fall, endless into the deadlight? When did I ever think it mattered? Because it doesn't. Nothing matters. I simply want this to end. But that's *my* want. And even that doesn't matter. And I'll get it in the end either way. So just go home.

It is with the residue of these spiralling ruminations and dancing considerations roiling through my mind that

I eventually find myself away from the city and back at the retreat, in my bed, after too many sleepless days, at last drifting off to sleep. Restless, though, the constant grinding of the gears holding stillness at bay, each question sparking the next, all cycling back to the beginning, repeating. I know that something is eluding me. That in the morass of noise, even if there isn't an answer, there is a thread that might lead to the question that might break the stasis. But what?

We've been here so many times before. It's what he does. What he's always done. How he's always been. I don't know why I ever loved him. Why did I love him? I loved him before… before *this*.

Before *humanity*.

Back at the dawn.

At the beginning…

The transition to sleep, and the dream, is in the end seamless. The question was never about me, or the current situation. It was always about him. About then. But what? What is it I need from him?

I go in search of him in the ancient lands that I prowled with my kind in the days before him. The earth back then was its own mistress – the ground and air, the flora and fauna, all uncontained, cycling, breathing, alive. Not the scarred and macadamised circus beast it has since become. In the dream my kind haunt the periphery, a sketched memory presence, much less than the very present group-self they were in actuality. In the dream they are a summary of a much more complicated truth, a truth I can only barely recall, and even then in just the broadest, vaguest of ways. In the dream I am the I that I have been for so long, as opposed to the all and part of the we that I once was. It has been so, so long since I have even considered that former self that it almost draws me away. But that is not for now. That's not why I am here. I am here for him. And I find him now where I found him then. In the treeline at the foot of his encampment.

Perhaps he heard me there, or smelt me. Perhaps he simply sensed me. Some lethal gravitational tug that drew him down from the safety of his kind, with their flint-head spears and stone-head axes, their skins and their fire pits. I don't know. I never knew. I never asked. He never told. How could we have lived so long together and never explored that first, impossible moment? And yet we never did.

He joined me in the trees that morning and he had no fear. Just fire in his eyes. Hunger in his belly, and in his loins. And power. A raw, muscular, torsional hunter. Fearless. Reckless. Impatient. Urgent. Mortal. His iron-thick blood thundering through veins that itched to hunt, to seize, to devour. And to fuck. No matter what it was that drew him to me, I know that what drew me to him was the animal that he was. The living, breathing, primal beast. How I wanted to touch him. Taste him. And, perhaps for just a moment, to *be* him. To walk in the shadow of his mortality and relish the inevitable end of it all, both without fear and with ferocious relish. To accelerate into it, through it, away from it, knowing that I would never escape it. How it must have felt to run through those trees with such utter oblivion forever snapping at one's heels. To live like that, every millisecond of that fleeting life worth infinitely more than all the assurances the certitude of my immortality bestowed upon me.

So we ran together. We chased and pounced. We fought and we fucked and saw everything through each other's eyes. And we saw each other. And we loved each other.

He became me, and I became him.

In those days we walked in the sun.

In those days we *were* the sun.

But it wasn't to last. I should have known. But I was consumed, lost in him, in this new, exhilarated, visceral paradigm of being. It was all my fault.

The screams came to us through the trees before dawn. Terrible, terrified, awful cries.

In my dream we sit up, as we did that morning, and we move without hesitation as we did then. And I know that in my bed I am weeping, as he did when we reached them, and as I didn't know how to until much later. In my dream we race back through the trees to his encampment, his people, and we find it as we found it then.

Not all of them were dead. Just the strongest – skewered and gutted, their faces mutilated into cruel mockeries of laughing terror, propped up like scarecrows in a ghastly theatre of death-as-life. The rest – the aged, the children, the nursing mothers – all bound and ablaze in a pyre at the centre of it all. Weeping and screaming. And throwing curses at him. Blame. Those who understood the concept of blame.

And those who didn't, the children mostly, throwing prayers at him. To be saved. To make the pain stop.

His mother was one of the ones burning. As were five of his brothers. And a sister. A little one. She had adored him. And he her. He listened to her skin crackle and pop as she died, his name sobbed over and over through blistered and blackening lips.

And, with dead eyes, from his position on a stick, his father watched him fail to save the family he had damned the moment he had followed me into the trees.

My kind had made their feelings on our courtship clear.

I watch him fall to his knees and tear at his hair as the sun rises behind the flames and looks down on him, his vengeful god in all its wrathful glory, transmuting flesh into law.

I struggle to remember how things went after that, but in my dream it is more than I can bear. It is more than I dare to imagine, what he must have borne.

It breaks my heart. It is unbearable.

And then the narrative of the dream diverges from the past. In my dream someone steps from the fire.

It is the boy. The boy with the dark skin. The one that he lives in now.

And I know that this is not a dream of him. It is actually him, here, in my dream. My dream terror and horror instantly turn into very real terror. *He* has found me. I am sure of it. Then the boy speaks. 'I am alone. He is with the others.'

'How are you here?'

'I'm not sure. When he is with the others, I can look around. There are pathways. Corridors. Rooms. Places. So many of them lead to here. The ones he walks the most. They all circle here. This fire. That sun. The Sun that Burns. That is what he calls it… it's what we all call it… isn't it?'

The boy looks confused and I suspect that he too is dreaming. And while a million questions radiate out from my conviction that our presence here in this place is fact, one monolithic truth assails me. That while I may have made him, he then went on to make us. His impossible, impervious, excruciating guilt and entrapment in this moment, fuelling millennia of guilt and loathing, exiling us all to the shadows, hiding us all from the Sun that Burns. Defining him. Defining us. Making us what we have become.

'Yes child. That is what we call it.'

The child then looks over his shoulder, eyes wide. 'He's coming back.'

'Go.'

'What should I do?'

'Wait for me. I will come for you.' And at the final moment the right question comes to me, at last: 'Do any of them ignore him? "*Feral rats*"? Has he found their leader yet?'

The boy nods. Yes. But he says nothing. He puts his finger to his lips and his eyes command silence. Then the sun and the pyre and the light detonate and I am thrown from the dream and back into the reality of the darkened room, and my tear-soaked pillow.

2

Happens every time.

Always some that are intransigent. Lawless. They fear no god. Not even me.

But there are ways. There are always ways.

Yet it's so much harder this time, with no corporeal presence to stand before them. No eyes with which to stare them down. No presence to communicate my alpha dominance to their beta insurgence.

Those first few days I concentrate on drawing in the obedient ones. Mostly the younger ones. A few of the older ones, the ones who will be missed by their parents. Who have never been in trouble before. The dull ones. I have them come to the rat nest where the rat-mother lives. I bring them in and cage them like the vermin they are. The mother retreats into her narcotic refuge and that's fine. Better that than her mewling and rocking and shaking and all the rest of it. As long as she doesn't die. I will need her to draw the son – and the fucking knife – home. All in good time. Rats always return to the nest, no matter how much they desire to escape it.

I had hoped that more would come. Situations like this are always a numbers game, and the numbers this time lean away from me. Tiresome. Not impossible. Just more work – more engagement – than I have the appetite for. There was once a time when I had appetite for nothing else. But no more. The material quality has dropped too far. The high not high enough. Dirty drugs. Dirty lives.

So – we have eleven of them here. Plus Danny and Peter. And out there perhaps twenty or thirty. It's hard to tell exactly. A lot of the connections are weak. Stuttering. And some of them huddle in small packs, making it hard to distinguish the individuals within them – formative group-think always blurs the lines. What they need is a ringleader. But leaders must lead. This is going to get messy before it can be cleared up.

His name is Ricky. Of the host of them out there, on the loose, paying the barest heed to my will, it is this Ricky that carries the most authority. And only with some of them. But enough of them. A gang. A singular, manipulable mass. Easy enough to turn it into a cause, give it gravity, draw them in. Make them an 'us', and set them against a 'them'. The poverty and hunger and hate gifted them by the world has already done half the work for me.

Over the first week or so I embed myself with Ricky and influence. His small pack continue to defer to him, and that is good. But their hunger is ferocious. Their aggression even more so. It is not as simple as minimising the collateral damage. If anything I have to exaggerate it, if only moment-arily. Burn bright, hard, fast. Out.

I send them out into the city to indulge their new-found appetites and urges. But I ensure they destroy, every time. No more spread of me into the morass. When they take, they kill, they devour every drop. And I have them target appropriately. The lonely and infirm. The vulnerable. Children are out of bounds – a shame really: every child destroyed at least being a life of pain spared – but the rats seem to care about them. Child-destruction mobilises them, and I'm not ready for their involvement. Not yet. In time I will need them to do what they always do when driven by fear of the *other* in their midst: segregate and destroy; but too soon and I will only disperse these plague rats of mine that I so need to congeal.

So a feast, in the beginning. Milk and honey for the faithful. The city spasms.

And then, as their hunger abates I have Ricky rise up in front of them. Speak to them. I prime him with the dialogue of the persecuted that has been recycled endlessly since the very dawn of them. I make him their prophet. And, their bellies full, their emergent sense of place taking hold, they listen. To him. Not to me. They don't need to listen to me. They just need to nod their solidarity with him in unison when I suggest it. Raise their fists in common cause upon my whispered insinuations. By the end of the second week the pack is knit, with Ricky at its core. And perhaps less than thirty deaths across the city is the price. Affordable. Not as dear as I'd anticipated.

Once bound, it's a simple case of rounding up the stragglers. In times gone past I might have considered an *omerta* – join or die – but it is not necessary this time. This time all I need is a clean core group. And so assassination is the assignation. Find the last few, bleed them. Enjoy it. Savour every drop. It is an easy sell.

So three weeks, nearly a month, and a semblance of order is created.

I divide my time between the nest and Ricky's battalion. The nest requires less attention. The rats there are fearful. Of the world. The sun. Me. They don't want to leave. They want to go home, but they know they have no homes. Not any more. Danny functions as an exemplary left hand. He observes and reports. His obedience is matched only by his natural aptitude and commitment to the cause. He of course has his own obvious motivations for wanting the knife-bearer, indeed his *murderer*, too. The desire for vengeance is always strongest in the unjustly condemned.

And so most of my time is spent with Ricky. The need for more constant, discrete manipulations is profound. These are caged pack-hunters. Itching at the leash. Scratching at the bars of their cage. *All in good time, my faithful… just wait… be patient… too soon would be too small*, I tell them. *We must plan. We will explode across the cruel consciousness of the world that holds us in penury.* Words to that effect – they don't have the vocabulary. The wonder of radicalisation is its capacity for delayed gratification on the promise of prophesied glory. Not a permanent solution, but a decent enough holding pattern.

All I need to do now is find the right location.

Somewhere I can bring them all together – the weaklings from the nest, together with Ricky's war party. And there I can let the massacre ensue and, as the numbers whittle away in that sealed abattoir, so my control over the remainder will reconstitute and increase exponentially. It will be glorious. And at the end of which I will be left standing with just one of them – I haven't yet decided which, possibly Danny – and I can get back to that final loose end.

The knife.

The ever-fucking knife.

3

Danny went into the bedroom and quietly clicked the door shut behind him.

The woman, the mother of his killer, looked up from her drugged sprawl on the bed and, after a moment's hesitation while the gears groaned into motion, sprang up and back against the wall. Her eyes widened and the tears came quickly. She said nothing.

Danny looked at her blankly as she adopted her terrified cower. Then he asked her: 'Do you love him?'

That threw her. Her eyes narrowed and her head tilted. A slight sneer, for just a second, as if a reflex action wanted to dismiss the question with some flavour of disdain – but her newly minted fear of this terrible child, with the monster living inside him, restrained her. 'Huh?' was all she could manage.

The boy moved into the room, deposited the pile of clothes that had been discarded on the moulded plastic garden chair onto the floor, and took a seat. He pulled his legs up in front of himself and hugged them, rested his cheek on his knee and regarded her balefully. There were tears in his eyes, and his bottom lip trembled. 'He's not here. The bad thing inside us. He's busy. He'll know if we do anything silly. But we can talk. Do you love him?' he said quietly.

His voice was different. Local. Like he was from here. Unlike the voice of the other one. Their master.

'Who?'

'Your boy. The one that killed me. John.'

'Of course I love him.' Another reflex response.

Danny tilted his head, and the corners of his mouth pinched in disbelief. 'Really? What's his favourite book?'

She looked away from him, shrugged and fished through her clutter for something to smoke. 'He doesn't really like reading.'

'His favourite film? TV programme? What does he like to do?'

She snorted at that. 'He likes being a little fucking shit is what he likes to do. That, and making my life even more difficult than it already is.'

'So you don't want him back?'

She didn't answer that. But she considered it, her body pausing momentarily from its usual twitch and fidget.

'Do you know what happened to your other boy? How he died? He was still awake when this thing inside me made me saw his hands off. Peter helped. Your boy wasn't in too much pain. Drugs. But he knew it was happening. I don't think he was still there when we took his teeth. But he might have been. It's hard to tell. I don't really understand these things.' The boy's voice broke at the end of that, and the tears started to fall when he repeated, 'I don't really understand these things.'

The woman looked across at him, her hand covered her mouth and she started to shake.

The boy cleared his throat, sat upright and pulled himself together: 'What do you suppose will happen to the other boy? To John? Do you think it will be so different? I try to imagine what it must have been like for your boy when we killed him. How confused he must have been. And scared. I think it must have been like when I died. When your other boy, John… when John killed me. I didn't *understand*. I was just… I was just going home, y'know? To my mum…'

He paused and shrugged and looked up into the corner of the room. He closed his eyes and the tears streamed freely. He made a low, awful keening sound.

'Mum is probably really worried. I guess. I don't know. See, I *know* she loves me. And I love her very much too.' He shook his head, opened his eyes, looked up at the ceiling, clenched his fists and thumped his thighs. 'This isn't fair.' He hissed.

Then he looked back at the woman on the bed, his eyes alive with rage and sadness and confusion: 'I want my mum,' he sobbed.

Something broke through with her then and she started to weep. 'Me too.'

'Does she love you?'

She rocked gently back and forth, turned her head to the side and whispered, 'I don't know. I don't think so. I don't know where she is. I don't really remember her.'

Danny frowned and nodded. He hopped down from the chair, moved round the bed to the window and pulled the tar-stained corner of the curtain back and peeped blankly out into the darkness of the concrete walkway outside and beyond to grim twinkling of the night-time city skyline.

'It's different in here to before.' He tapped his head. 'I'm not alone in here. There are pathways. *He* uses them, but I don't think he knows about all of them. He just knows the ones that join us to him. But there are paths everywhere. But they are like puzzles. Keyholes. You have to find combinations to open them up. It's a bit like that. But different. I haven't quite figured it out yet. The paths between all of us, his rats, are wide open. But the other paths need unlocking. I think when we're taken the pathways just open up... but the paths are there already. Just closed off. The paths... the *connections*... aren't made when we're infected. They're all already there. I don't think we *have* to infect each other to unlock them. I think maybe we can hack them. But I'm not sure. I've found a few old paths that go places he went before. Old places. Other people. I'm not sure who they are. Where they are. And I'm scared that he'll find out what I've found. I'm scared that he'll find out that I've been looking around.'

He turned back from the window and looked at her, his face open, asking her to be something she'd never been before. 'You are his mother. Your boy's mother. And he will die in the same way as your other boy. Probably in a worse way. And so will you. And me. All of us here. Even Peter. And Peter and I have already done that once. I don't want to do it again.'

'What can we do?' she asked. 'What can *I* do?'

Danny glared at her, his eyes flashing an instant of pure rage, his face tightening. He looked old. So, so old. He shook his head again and hesitated before muttering, 'I don't know. Maybe nothing. Maybe this will all just be what it will be. But I'm not going to just sit back and let it happen.'

She said nothing. Just watched him pace back and forth at the foot of the bed, his whole body locked in a posture of deep thought. The moment lasted for a minute or two, but it felt like hours to her. She didn't know what the boy wanted. And she struggled with thoughts clouded now by the stirred-up silt of the long-settled sludge of her deepest emotions and hurts. Then he stopped and said, 'I hate him, you know. What he's done.'

She nodded. 'Do you think you can stop him?'

Danny looked at her sharply then. 'Not *him*. Your *boy*. I *hate* him,' he growled.

She recoiled at the viciousness of his tone because she knew it was directed at her too, and, with or without the other thing inside him, she knew he was dangerous. That he too had power now. And a rapidly burgeoning capacity for intent. 'I don't care about *him*.' He tapped his head again. 'I *understand* him. But your boys. You. I *hate* you. I don't care what happens to you. If the same thing happens to you as happened to your other boy, fine. I don't care. It's just if it does, it will happen to me too. And I don't want it to happen to me. Or Peter. Or some of these others here. It's not *fair*. You... you *deserve* this. *You* have done this. I haven't done *any-thing*. Nor has my mum. It's not fucking fair.' He was roaring his words by the end of his tirade, and he stopped suddenly and turned towards the door. 'He hears me. I should go.'

He reached for the door-handle, turned it and pulled the door open. Then he stopped again. 'But you didn't answer the question.'

'What question?' she quavered.

'Do you love your boy?'

She thought of him then. Of when he had been little and had reached for her with affection and how, every now and then, he had received affection in return. Of his smile. Of the light in his eyes. Of her jealousy of that light. Her resentment. Of how much he made her hate herself because he'd loved her and she hadn't known how to love him back. And of how now, so late, too late, she realised that she'd loved him all along. And that she'd lost him. Long ago. And how much she missed him. How much she missed that light that she'd only seen fleetingly, like the passing of a comet, and whether she'd ever see it again. And then she thought of teeth bundled in ragged tissue and needles and sawn-off hands. She thought of all of these things and she crumbled into herself, and into her sadness, and she knew the awful answer to Danny's terrible question.

'Yes... yes... I love him... I do...'

Danny lowered his head at that, said nothing and stepped quietly from the room, closing the door silently behind him, leaving her with her tears and her loss and confusion, a mother at last, with no children left to mother.

Good.

CHAPTER EIGHT

SANCTUARY AND REJECTION

1

It was the smell of bread being baked that woke him. As it had done on a number of days since he'd come here. He opened his eyes and lay there, looking at the high ceiling with its decorative plasterwork bridging the corners where it met the walls. The small chandelier that hung above his large, soft bed was still dimly illuminated. He smiled.

Late-afternoon winter sun washed in through the tall sash windows that looked out over the busy garden, giving the room a salmon-pinkish hue that made him feel even warmer than his cosy bedroom already was. He wasn't tired. He felt good. In the weeks since the end of his old life and the beginning of this new one, he'd quickly learnt how it was to feel well.

The first week had been tough. There was no TV in the house. And they wouldn't let him smoke or drink. They let him have coffee with as much sugar as he wanted, but that was pretty much it. He'd wanted at first to go back to the block, but they'd told him it wasn't safe. That the ones who had his mother would be looking for him. He hadn't believed them. He didn't know why they wanted to keep him, but he couldn't conceive that anyone would be looking for him. He hadn't done anything. That's what he told them.

But they'd known. And they'd looked at him sadly. Sadly, because he lied to them. Sadly, because of what he'd done. He'd stabbed the boy. The man with the scar had seen him do it. And at first he denied it and swore and kicked and screamed and threatened to leave. But he couldn't. Because deep down he wasn't really sure he wanted to.

They started leaving newspapers out for him to see. He read with increasing concern as, over the weeks, the story of the boy he'd murdered – murdered! He simply couldn't believe it, he'd hardly touched him – kept moving progressively deeper into the journals, to ever-decreasing patches of real estate squeezed in between stories about speed cameras and publicity advertising cheap Christmas presents. The story was pushed back by ever more brutal murders, starting with the slaughter at the flat, where his brother had been the unknown victim of a ritualistic murder. Not that the papers knew it was his brother – but he did. John did. *They* told him. And he believed them. Once he'd got over his initial habitual disrespect and disbelief of all things authoritative.

So, the murder. Then *murders*. Then disappearing children.

The newspapers went wild. There was talk of cults and the decline of civilisation, the collapse of all virtue, the devaluation of existence, the end of love, the deification of death, the demise of morality and the death of God. All of these things. Yet none of them knew how to pin the tail on the donkey, the scarred man, the one they called Rider (some jokingly called him Joyrider, but John didn't get the joke) would say. Which was a good thing, for them. It was nothing more than Darwinian motion in action. A new top predator had evolved. But like over-aggressive, simple-minded viruses, it would burn itself out. And we will help it. And they will forget and they will all go back to their daily migrations from stable to workhouse and back. John wasn't sure what that was supposed to mean. But he quickly started believing them when they said that they would be looking for him. That the knife that had fallen into his possession was at the root of all this.

And they'd explained to him what it was they were. And they'd offered to let him join them. But he'd declined. For now. And they'd accepted that. Made no odds to them. He wouldn't be the only one. He'd be the youngest, by quite some stretch, but needs demanded. He'd needed protection. They'd brought him in.

Over the weeks his sleeping pattern had gradually drifted to align more with theirs. He'd awake every day, in his bed, in his room, to ever so slightly longer shadows running across the carpet from the treetops in the fields beyond. Not always to the smell of baking bread, but occasionally. More often it would be the smell of brewing coffee.

He felt safe. And he felt well. And the thrashing anger and sense of abandonment that had until so very recently lived inside him, and had indeed very much wagged the dog, slept. It was still there, he was quite sure of it, and he felt sure it always would be. But it was still, for now. And he would be its master. With their help. He would be his own master.

He swung his feet out from under the duvet and down onto the thickly piled carpet. He stood and scrunched his toes. It made him fizz all over. He walked across to the window and looked out across the garden. It was curious-looking. They'd explained that it was as it was for its smell. The colours that informed the landscaping of most gardens were of little interest to them. Night stripped the world of its colour. But not of its scent. And their sense of smell was keen. Which was why their garden was as it was. He'd not had much experience of gardens, and so wouldn't have noticed if they hadn't mentioned it to him. But now that it had been pointed out, it was a fact that he liked to chew over when he woke up and looked down on it. It intrigued him. That these things are thought about at all. That the geometry of the world would sometimes bend to accommodate such thought. He wondered where else this might be the case. If perhaps the geometry of the world wasn't in fact bent out of shape everywhere mankind existed. The thought was as big as any thought he'd ever had. As were many of the thoughts he was having these days.

Life was different now.

Life was good.

He smiled.

He could see activity down by the barns where the pigs spent their nights. The day crew finishing up their chores. They said when everything had calmed down he might be able to help out down there too. But for now, it wasn't worth the risk.

He made his way down to the basement, to the huge communal kitchen and dining space that occupied the area between the foot of the basement stairs and their bedrooms. The radio was on quietly. Some old man talking about some history stuff with other old men and a younger-sounding woman. It was soothing to hear, just the sound of interested voices engaged in conversation. He took in none of what they were saying. No one was up other than the one who had brought him here, who was waiting for him.

'Hello John. How did you sleep?'

John smiled and nodded and pulled himself up onto a stool at the breakfast bar.

'Bread will be ready soon. Would you like a coffee?'

'Yep.'

The man, Rider, raised an eyebrow.

'Please,' John finished.

Rider took down a heavy mug from a hook above the kitchen counter and poured some coffee into it from a filter jug. He placed the cup down in front of John and looked at him seriously. 'We need to start sorting things out.'

'What things?'

'The things you've been reading about in the paper. The people who are looking for you.'

John shrugged insolently. 'Don't see why.'

'I'm sure you don't. And I don't really care if you see why or not. Doesn't change the fact that it's now time to act.'

John was unsure of the man's tone. There was something beneath it. Something that hadn't been there before. Something hard. John didn't like it. And he responded like he always had. Badly. 'You think you can tell me what to do? You think a few days in your fancy fuckin' house with your bread and shit and I'm gonna just do what you want me to do?'

'You are going to do what you have to do to put right everything that you have made wrong.'

John jumped down from his stool at that and snarled up at his host, 'I ain't done nothing. You can fuck off. You don't know me. What the fuck do you know about what I done?'

'You know already that I know precisely what you've done. You've killed a child. And you've unleashed a plague. And now you're going to help me clear up your mess.'

'Or what?'

Rider glared at the child for a short moment and then simply laughed kindly at him. 'Oh John. You know that the options are endless. We could dine on you tonight instead of one of the pigs. How about that? I could just put you out and send you away. But you know we won't. No. If you don't help me I'll just have to send you home.'

'I won't go.'

The man swept up the mug and poured the untouched coffee down the sink. He watched it swirl down the plughole and talked softly over his shoulder. 'You'll go wherever we decide to put you, John. Whether you stay there or not will indeed be entirely up to you. But they're all looking for you. You have something they want, you see? They want it more than anything. And they'd do anything to get it. They'd do anything to make you tell them where it is. And they'd probably do even more if you told them you didn't know where it was.' The man ran the cold tap for a moment to rinse the sink, shut it off, turned and dried his hands on a tea towel. 'You've read the papers. You know how they do things.' He shrugged casually. 'Up to you.'

John was new to all of this. New to being stood up to. New to having nowhere to run to. New to responsibility. Cause and effect. He wasn't very good at it. He was scared. He wasn't new to that, but he was new to admitting it. But he didn't need to admit it. Rider knew. And he had John over a barrel.

'Do you think it will all just go away if you don't do something about it?'

John looked down at his hands. 'No. I just don't know what I'm supposed to do.'

'What do you think you have to do?'

'I don't know!' He wailed. 'I just know I don't want to go back. I don't ever want to go back.'

Rider walked across to the child and put his hand on his shoulder. 'I never said you had to go back.'

'Then what? What do I have to do?'

The man put a phone in his hand. 'Don't you think it's time you called home? Told your mother you're alright?'

John looked up at him like he had completely lost the plot.

Rider shrugged at the boy again, then nodded. 'Maybe tell her you love her?'

2

It's been three weeks since he's gone and she almost believes it's true. It's been three weeks of ever-increasing fear and confusion out there on the estate, but she's more or less immune to all that. She almost thinks she's lucky. She'd had her hope pretty much extinguished from the get-go. They'd told her that her boy was dead and he hadn't disappeared until a few hours after that. By that point she'd already accepted that he was gone. That they'd lost his body was now neither here nor there. There was plenty she didn't understand. Plenty more she didn't *want* to understand. Nothing seemed real any more.

The first forty-eight hours had been the toughest. But she wonders if perhaps they were the toughest because all eyes were on her. And not all of those eyes had been sympathetic. Some of those eyes were looking to see if she'd had something to do with it. Because dead boys don't disappear from hospitals. It was suspicious. And so there were whispers. But the deep swell of fear that had since swallowed the estate had absorbed any whispers directed at her and her boy. They quickly lost interest in the wake of what had followed.

The disappearances. And the deaths.

They'd asked her a lot of questions at the outset – police, family, friends, neighbours – but had quickly become distracted by more recent developments. They'd moved on. And the world had whipped itself up into a panic. The city was losing its mind. But these things didn't trouble her. They didn't touch her. They were happening in a different world. A million miles away. And that was fine by her.

Because her boy was gone and he wasn't coming back.

She knew it. She knew it the moment they'd told her he'd been hurt.

They'd arrived at the door and asked to come in. She'd looked at them, their grim faces, and she'd known. She'd shown them into the sitting room and had gone through to the kitchen and taken the pan of water off the heat. She'd turned off the gas that was frying the onions. They'd not be having bolognaise tonight. They'd not be having bolognaise ever again. She knew it. She knew it. She knew it.

She'd turned off the cooker and counted to ten. Then she'd turned and gone through to hear them. One of them had been standing sombrely in front of the TV, the other one perched on the edge of the sofa, hat and hands in lap. They'd told her straight out. Hadn't minced their words. They were very professional. And she'd appreciated that. As much as she could appreciate anything. She'd pulled her lips between her teeth, gently bitten down, held her composure, and had asked them where he was.

They'd explained, and she'd asked them to take her to him. Then she'd got her coat and checked the lights were off before they left the flat.

He'd been gone by the time they got there.

Which was when the questions really started. Where was his father? Did she have any boyfriends? Was he being bullied? Had he mentioned anything to her? They hadn't kept her too long. She'd told them she was tired and could she go home now?

She hadn't turned any lights on when she'd got in. She'd gone through to her room, in her coat and her shoes, and she'd lain on the bed and looked at the ceiling. She hadn't cried. She barely even made a sound. She tried not to breathe. She tried not to blink. But in the end her body would oblige her. That's just the way it was built. She felt guilty about that. Eventually she got tired, and eventually she slept. She'd felt guilty about even countenancing the idea of sleep, but it had crept up on her in the end and taken her away from it all. She hadn't dreamt.

When she'd awoken there had been a few moments when it had all been a dream. A heavenly interlude of untruth, swaddling her in the beautiful notion of her boy not being dead. It had been her shoes that had shattered that moment. The shoes still on her feet. On her bed. They were the vicious little detail that moored her to reality. It had been her shoes that had appropriately repositioned her existence from hope to despair and had reset the trajectory of her life ever since. It had been her shoes that had calibrated the sine wave of her grief. Set in motion the pendulum of her pain.

But she hadn't cried. She'd retreated into a middle distance somewhere between presence and detachment and she'd operated herself remotely from there.

She'd gone through to his room and sat on his bed and looked at his bookshelf. *Harry Potter. Asterix* and *Tintin.* And a tiny part of her blamed them. The books. Because if he hadn't been into his books, he would have been somewhere else, somewhere other than between the library and here, and it wouldn't have happened.

Over the coming weeks she thought about keeping a note of the things she found to blame. Because they were bizarre. She thought that maybe one day she'd look at that list and it might make her smile. That perhaps it might help someone else get through this. Maybe she could write a book. Maybe she could keep a list of the crazy things she could do to get through this. Like writing a book.

She didn't keep a list. She didn't write a book. She never thought a day would come. Every day was every day and they were all the same because he wasn't there and the pendulum swung and the sine wave waved and she just rode it on through, immune to the tumult and horror that was washing up at her front door. Safe in her bubble of numb.

And now it's been three weeks. It's been three weeks.

It's been three weeks since her boy was taken, since the world turned into a different world. And yet still she needs bread and milk. Other things too. How can the world no longer have him in it, and yet still consider a need for bread and milk not absurd? How could her body contain so much sadness and still find room for bread and milk? She should write that down. She doesn't. She puts on her coat and she heads out to the shop. For bread and milk.

She drifts through the tight walkways and underpasses like a phantom, a barely there shadow in the grander scheme of things. She is outside of time, and very nearly outside of space. A subatomic particle inhabiting the gaps between the grinding actualities of the urban machine. At the shop she doesn't see the papers. The headlines. The cruel accrual of lost children and ragged corpses. She doesn't see. She doesn't care. She is elsewhere.

Coming back from the store is the same, but in reverse. The empty carrier bags she'd taken with her – ever conscientious: always re-use – are now half full with the barest of essentials. Enough to see her through today. Maybe even tomorrow. Assuming there is such a thing.

It is in the stairwell where he died that it happens.

She has had to walk past the flowers laid there every day since they'd come to her door with the news. Not as many flowers as one might have expected. There would probably have been more had subsequent events not overtaken his demise. Stolen his moment in the jet-black spotlight. But the early adopters had got in there early and a few bunches of extended condolences still lay at the scene. Her eyes had seen them, day in, day out, but there'd been no connection. Nothing had reached her.

But today she stops, and she sees them. And this time something stings her, a feeling crashes through, and for a moment the fog lifts and the agony of her loss is exposed in all its terrible glory. She looks at the flowers, wilting on the floor where her boy bled out, and she sees herself, and what she has become. What she is without him. She sees herself as an echo of a memory of a fleeting inspiration, so much less than once she was, with so much more to never do, and so much time to spend pretending that she is anything at all.

She has spent so much time resisting the impetus to examine his pain in his last moments, to explore, perhaps even to taste, the fear he must have felt, the beautiful innocence that probably insisted on telling him everything would be fine, that she has missed her own pain. Her own overwhelming and all-consuming sadness.

Because *she* didn't die in the stairwell with blood on her trousers. *She* didn't wonder what was happening when the world drifted into the glooming and abandoned him. No. *She* is still here, along with everyone else, just another bunch of failing memories and aspirations, a ruined vessel of hope and beauty. Just like the flowers here in the stairwell, like every black-spot bouquet, she was trying to feign relevance in the wake of what went before, and what went before was just as pointless.

She breaks then.

Her chin wobbles.

She turns and runs up the stairs and fumbles with her keys. She lets herself in and falls back against the door, slides down it. The milk and the bread wait patiently beside her.

And she weeps, and she wails, and she thinks of her boy, and understands that he is gone. And that she will never have bolognaise again.

And neither will he.

3

Anna sat on the bench and waited for the boy.

John hadn't come home as they'd thought he would. He'd phoned. And he'd known they were there. That had been a surprise. Not a good one. And it had taken weeks.

He'd spoken briefly to his mother and then asked to speak to them. He'd told them that he knew what they wanted. But that he wanted something in return. That was the only way they'd get the knife. And that if he didn't get what he wanted, he'd take the knife to Ricky, and his horde of infected rats.

He said he wanted his mother back.

And that if he got her back he might let things lie.

Filthy little rat-child. Disgusting little upstart.

He knew too much. Wanted too much. How did he know so much?

He would have to die. And he would. As would his mother.

Just as soon as they had the knife.

And so they'd agreed to meet him at the bench in the park. *The* bench.

His suggestion.

They didn't like it.

But what choice did they have?

So here was Anna, sitting in the light of the lamp, waiting for the child.

The sky was clear. Stars were out. The moon, half full, hung low in the sky. A fine ground mist blurred across the grass of the field. She sat there and she waited.

Nothing. He was late.

She didn't think he'd come. But she had to wait. She had her instructions.

Someone approached the bench from across the grass. She squinted her eyes, sharper now than ever before, but nonetheless delivering information that didn't fit her expectations. The person heading towards her was an adult. Male. The possible hint of a limp. Couldn't tell. Probably just a dog-walker.

She looked left, and then right. No sign of the child. She looked at her watch.

He's not coming.

Wait.

She started to fidget. And worry. Something.

The man approaching across the grass stepped into the outer circle of the light and stopped. He looked across the path at Anna, his hands behind his back. She looked at him, didn't recognise him, and then continued her watch of the path. He had an ugly scar running into his hairline from his cheek.

The man smiled quietly to himself and continued across the path and sat on the bench next to her. She locked eyes with him, and told him in no uncertain terms that it would be in his best interest to move along.

His response threw her: 'You don't recognise me, my sweet?' A smirking sadness in his eyes.

She reiterated her advice for him to move along. That he had no idea what she was capable of. And that she was not there for whatever it was that he thought she might be there for.

He turned away his face, looked out across the field and repeated his question. But this time he used the old language.

Anna stiffened, her whole body possessed then by the old-one who sent her there. Her face a broiling stew of disbelief, incomprehension, betrayal and grief. The man looked back at her then: 'There you are.' He smiled softly at her and sighed.

She turned sharply then and looked out across the empty space of the park. There were tears in her eyes. She managed one word: 'Why?'

The man looked down at his hands and shook his head. 'What choice did you leave me? What should I have done?'

'You should have stayed with me.'

'Why?'

'Because I needed you. Because you were all I had.' Her cry echoed dully through the mist.

'Needed me for *what*? What was the plan? Walk the earth hating it until it fell into the sun? Why did you need me for that? We can fall into the sun whenever we want. Why wait?'

The thing inside Anna had no answer for that.

The man straightened up and looked out into the middle distance. 'How many of them are here? How many are watching us? I can see the baby over there. That's the same place I watched you from when you rose. Tried to rise.'

Anna stood and turned, her eyes narrowing viciously, 'You watched? You *watched*?!'

The man shrugged. 'I had to make sure. I wasn't sure you'd do it. I was actually quite proud of you. It had been a while.' He raised his hand then, an immediate apology for the low blow. It wasn't necessary, however true it might have been. 'But that's not why we're here.'

Anna laughed bitterly at that. 'Why *are* you here? What do you *want?*'

'I want to help you clear up this mess…'

'… which you helped create…'

'… which I helped create. Yes. I did. I created this mess when I created you. You are my mess. You've been my mess for too long. And you are still my mess. But we're going to do this my way, and then you are going to *rise*. And that will be that. This is the end, for us.'

Anna looked at him in disbelief. 'And you couldn't have done it this way in the first place?'

'Maybe. If I hadn't been so scared of you. But I was. Not any more.'

'So you set me up to burn? You burn yourself? What else don't I know?'

'Plenty. And there's plenty more you will continue not to know, because we are done.'

Anna's eyes flashed lightning-blue at that and she leapt at his throat with a roar. The man moved quickly, up and out of the way. Anna is slow. Slower than the shadow inside her might be used to.

'I wouldn't. If anything happens to me, the knife goes to *them*. Do you understand me?'

Anna took a deep breath and got herself under control. 'What do you want?'

'I want the boy's mother. I want her alive and well. Unharmed. And then I will work with you to stop them.

And once that is done, I will deal with the knife, and I will deal with you. And we can all move on.'

'How can I trust you? After all this? How can I know you won't betray me again?'

Anna looked up at him from the bench where she'd landed after her fruitless lunge. He looked down on her from the far side of the path and proffered an expression familiar to every spurned lover back to the dawn of time, 'Why would you think I would want to keep you around after everything I've done? I thought I was free of you, and yet here you are. All over the place, as bad as you ever were. I want you *gone*. I've wanted you gone for so long now. So I will help you. Do you understand?'

Anna pulled her knees up to her chest and threw her arms round them, and a small sob escaped her. 'You said you loved me.'

The man turned and started to walk back across the grass, back into the darkness.

'I did.'

'You lied.'

'We all lie.'

'I love you.'

'You don't even know what love is.'

Anna watched him fade away into the darkness. A jogger rounded the corner on the path below the bench. She could hear the beat pumping from his headphones, even from this distance.

The man's voice called out from the darkness, making her jump. 'Don't bother sending them after me. You're not as fast as you used to be. Keep the mother indoors and look after her. We'll be in touch.'

And with that he was gone.

The jogger thumped past the bench and spared her the briefest sideways glance.

Anna wiped a sleeve across her cheek, stood and followed in the runner's wake.

She didn't have the knife.

She didn't have the boy.

But she knew that the old thing that was haunting her, as it receded back into the cloud that now demanded so much of his attention, was weaker than she'd previously thought.

And she wavered.

She wavered.

CHAPTER NINE

CALCULATIONS AND CHAOS

1

They'd been watching him for forty-eight hours now, and
there were still gaps in the story. They couldn't link him
to every murder scene they'd encountered, but they could
tie him to some of them. And the pins in the map in the
investigation room were thickest around Ricky's address,
and seemed to orbit out from there. That the flurry of
violence was gang-related was beyond anyone's doubt. But
how some of the victims had got themselves caught up
in it was beyond most of their ken. A few of the victims
fitted the profiling spectrum, but most of them just seemed
innocent bystanders. After years of this kind of violence
being primarily drug-related – with perpetrators and victims
by and large falling somewhere within the description of
'buyer' or 'seller', and by extension fairly generic, not to

mention depressing, race and age parameters – this was different.

But at first no one could agree on what that difference meant, and that had cost them time, and it had probably cost lives. The sheer level of the violence, the literal blood-letting glee, not to mention the bizarre absence of blood that the scenes presented indicated a mind gone terribly wrong. But as the days progressed and the crimes multiplied, it became clear that more than one person was involved. That it was some kind of collective mania. And that had more in common with a nascent protection racket, in that the primary connective tissue seemed to be geographical proximity to a specific location. But, as a vocal minority mumbled quite audibly, protection usually did involve some degree of actual, y'know, *protection*. This didn't.

At first they wondered how the missing kids might be caught up in this. The initial fear of course was that they'd been killed. But CCTV footage unearthed a couple of them, out, late into the night. And then the patterns started to coalesce, but to nothing more than a blurred insinuation that the children might perhaps somehow have a more hands-on involvement. No one wanted to believe that the children were actually doing it themselves. But nobody was naïve enough these days to believe that kids weren't capable of terrible things. That kids weren't in fact monsters anyway, given half the chance. But again, too many loose ends. They couldn't figure out where the kids were. They'd pop up on camera, individually, occasionally, indicating that they weren't dead or locked up, and then they'd lose them again.

And so initially, in that first week, it had exploded and accelerated, like an outbreak of chickenpox. It was everywhere all at once on the estate. In the second week it started to plateau. No more disappearances. And the murders seemed to alter slightly. They started to appear more considered. Less driven by some kind of animal madness. More traditionally human. But no less sloppy. These weren't professional murders. Clues were found. Bits and pieces. Geographical indicators pointed inwards, and enough circumstantial evidence found at the scenes soon gave them a clear enough idea that, by week three, and following a timely tip-off, they were closing in on Ricky.

They were all too aware that if he committed some other atrocity while on their watch there would be hell to pay. A cautious few opposed storming his flat and hauling him in. Too risky – there was still too much they didn't know and they figured that they should follow his movements, find out what the hell was going on. But that was argued against because his name had popped up too many times now and he couldn't be left on the loose. They would storm into the flat, bring him in and get answers from him. What could possibly go wrong? But they would never get answers from him.

Of course they only knew as much as they did because I told them.

Because I tipped them off.

And it was all engineered anyway. Creating a radicalised cell, with its own rabid prophet. A fattened lamb. It is all part of the plan.

So the time had come, and I gave Ricky to them.

It is amazing how effective the anonymous tip-off can be. A number-withheld call to the right person can work like a spark onto warm, dry sawdust and *whoosh*. Away we go.

In the bedlam within the investigation, Anna's absence has been very low-priority. I've no doubt that Tom probably shared his clear concerns that she'd crumbled and sloped off. The messages on her phone, the disquiet in his voice suggest something greater than worry, whispering his belief that she'd lost it. No one else came searching. They are too busy looking elsewhere. Even Tom seems to have got caught up in it himself because the voicemails have petered out. But they haven't blocked her remote access. Why would they? And so I have observed their movements, their blundering circling in on something of which they have no understanding. Their chasing of their tails. I have watched and I have waited until their blurred triangulations gave me a minefield into which I could deposit Ricky.

Three weeks, thereabouts. Three weeks.

Rats: they have no idea how to hunt. It's embarrassing.

And so now they are watching him, with their fingers on their triggers.

Everything is set.

I wake him up at sundown. It's as much as I can do. Split as I am across so many now, my influence is debilitatingly weakened.

I have been lucky with Anna – she has been sympathetic. Enough. She shares my disgust. Enough. She has worked with me. But Ricky barely even registers my existence. I am the whining of an absent parent to him. And only when the charging clatter of his own directionless hatred and rage isn't drowning me out. I can place the occasional thought in his mind, and that is about it. And that is how it is with most of them. These rats, more animal even than the dog had been. More feral. If I am to shepherd them all to *her* – now *him*, with the scarred face – I need them united. As one. They need bringing together.

And so I whisper to him, 'They're here. They're coming for you.'

He sits bolt upright, eyes wide. He stands and goes across to the plywood drawers that are built into the alcove in the corner of the room. He pulls open the top drawer and takes out a sock that has something heavy inside it. He turns his head to the door and listens. He thinks he can sense them. Of course he can sense them. He can sense them through me. I am his sixth sense. But he thinks it is *he* that senses them. He thinks he is magnificent. He thinks he is invincible. And that is fine. That is perfect in fact.

'Ricky…?'

Her. The skinny rat-girl from next door. His pet now. She stirs and asks him what's up. Her I can't reach, reception too weak. Because I am in her through him. The family bond weakening with each generation. I can feel her as dull sound through a stretch of murky water. She knows nothing of me. She is herself, with my hunger. But essentially she is just herself. Gifted. Perhaps now with a dash of him, Ricky. Disgusting.

He shushes her with two words: 'They're here.'

'Who?'

He looks at her and smiles. I suggest to him that now it is time for him to rise. To rise to glory. To reveal himself to them, the new and mighty him. To let them know him, know what he has become. Yes. Let them know what it is they face.

He nods and heads to the door.

He pulls it quietly open.

The outer hallway is quiet and dark. He can smell the decay behind the door opposite, where he and the girl had first broken bread together and feasted on those old fatling rats. He smiles at the memory. The police don't have a pin in their board for them. He doesn't know how he knows this, how he even knows that they have a board, or how he can picture it in his mind. In here. He can't see it, not as he can see some things, but he *can* imagine it. He can smell them continuing to rot in there, that particular pin still in the tray. As are so many more. He is privy to knowledge now. Or so he thinks.

Herding rats is like that. They are so quick to believe they are more gifted than they are. It is easy enough for me to pass their secrets across the horde and to allow them to form their own ideas, make their own decisions based on knowledge I choose to share with them. And to then gently steer them to where they need steering. Anna's not seen the board this time round, but she has seen it before. She knows how it works. And now, so does he.

I've done it before. Rounded up a rabble. Long ago now.

She – not Anna, *she* – helped me on that occasion too.

Damn her. If she hadn't left me…

Ricky frowns. A bubble of sadness. He shakes his head and creeps out, across the darkened space, pulls open the fire door, dances through and scuttles up the stairs and out towards the front of the building. The images running through his verminous mind paint a tapestry of insurrectionist grandeur: he will explode out into the world and take down those who might think they have the power to bring him low. To send him back to his sewer. The fire in his mind is largely his own, I simply fan it, and the smoke and the heat obliterate any caution that the fear and oppression of poverty and worthlessness might up until now have quelled. He is primed, the pin pulled.

He peers out through the graph-paper glass of the front door and sees the darkness. No one milling about. It's been quieter out of late. He pulls the door open and steps out, brazenly, the sock in his hand doing nothing to conceal the gun contained within. It'll mask his fingerprints. But that will be moot.

He hears them. He smells them. He almost feels he can see them.

Someone shouts, 'Drop the weapon! Down on the floor!'

He smiles up at them and shows them his teeth.

'Drop it now!'

Red dots appear on his chest. They flicker across his eyes.

He looks down at his chest, then back up. He looks up into the sky, and breathes deeply through his nose. He prepares himself now to stand tall as their bullets bounce off him as he shoots back at them and, one by one, goes from throat to throat devouring them. He closes his eyes and savours the moment. The calm before the storm.

Then he lowers his face, starts to raise his gun.

The police don't hesitate. A short, sharp tattoo of gunfire, and Ricky's head and chest explode in unison.

He falls to the ground.

One down.

2

They settled like crows in the playground and murmured their outrage. Their pale eyes and scrawny, track-suited frames hunched, hands stuffed in pockets. They assembled. And this night brought not just the gifted together, but the ungifted too – the infected and the uninfected, united in their hatred for *them*. The pigs. The filth. And all that they represented. Their casual authority to swoop in and destroy, as they had destroyed Ricky, out there, right in plain view of everyone. So that they'd all know just who was in charge. What else could such an action be, *other* than a provocation?

But what to do?

They milled and fomented and kicked at the woodchip that was left on the bed of torn and exposed canvas that clothed the foundation of the tired playground equipment. Some of them smoked and drank. But many of them didn't. Many of them didn't do that any more. They were different now. They were *of a kind*. And this was new to them. It made them feel powerful. Empowered. Like they could do something about things.

But what? What to do?

Having lived entire lives in mute ignorance of the existential penury in which they were imprisoned, and in which they were destined to live out their days, battery-farmed, hen-pecked and regarded as the putrid Petri dish from which all social disease and disorder would germinate – something had now awoken in them. There was now something in them that was disgusted by them. And it came from out there, not here. Out there – where the police came and did something if you got robbed. Out there – where they went to school and got jobs and had aspirations that were attainable. Out there – where they hated our words and our music and everything about us.

Out there where people didn't get shot on their doorsteps.

Out there where they thought of them as rats.

But the rats could smell the poison now. Their little noses twitching. Their eyes glinting. Their bellies growling. They formed their petty playground parliament and they muttered and discussed and tasted disgust. They spat and made schemes fuelled by seditious mistrust. And there was a voice whispering in their ears. Needling them. Fuelling their conviction of the new dawning truth – of where they fitted into the scheme. What life had mapped out for them. How much they were worth.

Nothing.

They were worth as much as Ricky. Blown apart like a dangerous dog.

They were going to be destroyed for being what they were. That was how this script was being written. By the pigs. By the government. By their parents. By the old fucks who ran the world and hated them. By everyone who wasn't them and didn't understand what it was like never to have lived a single day that mattered. That hadn't been sullied by some casual meanness, cruelty or simple disregard or neglect. They had lived their whole lives and taken it – the hate, the neglect, the blame – and they'd never bitten back.

Why?

Because they were cowardly rats. And that's what rats did: steal from each other and scuttle around in the shadows scrabbling over scraps and dodging the poisons and traps and hurled objects that were unleashed to crush or kill them. Isn't it? Aren't they? Well?

They chorused their vehement opposition to the notion. And cawed their dissonant dissent. They hopped to their feet and started to flap their little wings. Then, as one, they took flight and swooped into the city. And there were enough of them that none stood in their way, and as they flocked through the streets, heading towards the police station where they knew Ricky's girl was now caged, their numbers grew. Others joined them. Others who had nothing, and wanted to show that they had nothing.

When they arrived at the police station a crowd had already formed, loudly but peacefully remonstrating with a senior police officer who had ventured out to speak to them on the steps. He obfuscated and avoided giving answers and wouldn't explain what evidence they had that might justify the shooting. There was a mother in the crowd, and she was wailing. There were uncles and cousins and neighbours and the like and they wanted to know why, after weeks living in terror of whatever had been stalking their estate, ripping out throats, they now had police in the shadows shooting at them too. The policeman was disinclined to make the connection for them – that Ricky was what had been terrorising them – it wasn't that clear-cut yet. But the crowd heard the insinuation nonetheless. They were disinclined to believe it, but not necessarily because it was beyond belief. He'd been no angel after all.

The new arrivals on the scene heard the insinuation too, and the gifted few among them knew it to have merit. But they also heard a veiled threat in his words: we've killed Ricky. We've caged his partner. We're coming for the rest of you next and we will destroy you just like we destroyed him.

It was all they needed.

A small group of them broke away from the main crowd. They tore from the ground a short metal post that bore a small parking restrictions notice and stove it through the window of a nearby police car. Some of the younger members of the crowd cheered at that and migrated across to this more proactive assembly. A teenage boy who was sipping from a half-litre bottle of vodka that was being passed around poured what was left through the hole in the windscreen and theatrically flicked a cluster of burning matches in after it. It went up with a whoomp.

The suited senior officer who had been on the steps quickly retreated back into the building. A number of the crowd who'd been demanding answers from him berated these scene-stealers who were smashing the police car, but quickly backed down when they saw the cold sparkle in the eyes lurking beneath the hoods. These ones had crossed a line. These weren't their children any more. They were something else. Their smiles were altogether too toothsome. Their intent less clear. More dangerous.

And whoomp, the next car went up. The less sober, ungifted kids then danced round the flaming vehicles, whooping and hollering and waving their hands in the air. A stream of riot police filed out of the station and assembled on the steps. They formed a line. The lippy kids cheered and started to throw bottles and cans and anything else that came to hand.

The gifted ones didn't. They swooped forward as one at the police line. The crowd of peaceful complainants had dissipated and things were about to get ugly.

The police crouched slightly and leant forward to meet the surging flock. They raised their shields and started to move down the steps towards them. Their attackers accelerated and smashed into them. What happened then made little sense to most of those who witnessed it. It was so fast, and so blurred, but the police were quickly dismantled and left broken and strewn across the street.

The crows looked down on their scattered foes and then started up the steps.

There was a moment of hushed awe from the kids at the burning cars, followed by a sudden swell of triumphant cheering. The traditional narrative – handed down from generation to generation for such a long stretch of history that it was now almost ingrained in their DNA – that they would be crushed by the powers that be was being rewritten before their very eyes. The noise and the spectacle and wildfire whispers of the changing of the guard, of victory and liberation, pulsed outward across the instant-message grapevine.

It was the perfect storm.

Three or four of the crows then charged into the station while the remainder circled and wheeled outside, keeping watch. Over the next minutes a few police staff threw themselves headlong out of the building, running for their lives. They ran directly into the circle of crows, who casually picked them off and laid them down alongside their fallen colleagues. A few moments after that the small group that had ventured in stepped back out into the throng with the girl from the cell – Ricky's girl – the closest thing they had to a queen. The martyr's wife.

The baying mass howled with valedictorian glee. They howled at the stars and the moon and the street lights and the cameras. They danced and they ran and they smashed. Across the city they heard the rising wail of sirens circling in to meet them and they grinned. Fresh meat. Lambs to the slaughter.

Then they lit out into the night.

They took the children with them.

And together they would bring the city to its knees.

3

It quickly metastasises into something more than I'd anticipated. More than I'd planned. We'd needed them to come together so that we could draw them out. We'd needed to unify them so that we could herd them. Sacrificing Ricky had been a necessary evil. It saddened me, but his cruelty and his hunger weren't *purely* symptomatic of his new condition. He was one of the bad ones, and so of all the ones to let go, he was the one. He was the one who had drawn the most attention, committed the most vicious acts. He hadn't been the head. The mob had been headless. But in the absence of a head, he had been the closest thing to the horde's controlling animal instinct. Its louder, uglier, nature. And he'd needed extinguishing before he made any of the others in his image.

But his death had served this secondary purpose. With a little gentle prodding, his death had become a rallying point for the latent disaffection that gilded the very cells of this new young clutch. It had unified them and caused them to flock. And as a flock we'd been able to steer them en masse. First to the police station to reclaim the girl. I'd insisted upon that. I'd told *him* no knife unless he brings them all. Every last one of them.

I would have preferred less violence in her rescue. Fewer deaths. But the deaths of some drones in uniform who could so casually threaten and shoot these children, whose causes for complaint far outweighed anything the drones and their paymasters themselves might present as counter-arguments – well, it was a small price to pay. And it wasn't without its own cruel symmetry.

Evolution's rough-hewn ingenuity, impressive as it clearly was, had still to find an answer to the conundrum of the omelette and the broken eggs.

So they had come together and they had flocked, and they had rescued the girl. Now they were coming to me. As had been the plan all along: he would round them up and then deliver them unto me and mine, and I would deal with them. I would enlighten them. And matters would be resolved.

But where reality was now dramatically deviating from the plan was in the secondary and tertiary conflagrations that the primary heat of our flock's rage was igniting as it passed. The latent disaffection that we'd used as leverage in the wake of Ricky's death wasn't unique to our small band. It was endemic. And our small uprising was now inspiring brainless facsimiles across the city. Children were rising up. Parents too. Many of the parents were in fact still children. Some of them weren't. But all of them had been, and if they didn't still feel the same way themselves, they remembered all too bitterly a time when they did. Pockets of unfocused anger, bubbling and rising up. Breaking stuff. Smashing, burning, looting, taking. That was how it started. But then even that spilt over into something else. A beige-white noise of lawlessness that said nothing, proved nothing. But spoke volumes. To anyone who might choose to hear. Of which there were few.

But the narrative wasn't really that complicated: when an individual can find no worth to assign to their own life, then what value is there in life itself? When there is nothing to lose, and perhaps nothing even to gain, then why not just lash out? Take... break... Howl at the world and not make a point because there was no point to be made. There was no point. That was the *whole* point.

Burn the world down to the ground? Why ask 'why', when the real question is 'why not'?

All it takes is for someone to go first. And for enough others to follow.

They had nothing. This proved it.

Every avalanche starts with a single snowflake that carries the mass across a critical threshold. It's that one straw too many that breaks the camel's back. It's just a single butterfly that needs to flap its wings for a tornado to flatten the world.

So, it transpires, was the case with Ricky.

The snowflake, the straw, the butterfly. And as the tornado gears up through the backstreets and alleys of the ghettos and starts to cascade across into the heart of the city, as shop windows cave in and looters run amok, as police huddle and charge and retreat and redeploy, our darling crows march on ahead to the prearranged location.

I await them, my own flock positioned at key vantage points along the way. They are heading in on the whispered promise of a leader, someone who can explain their condition and utilise their gifts. Someone who will show them a path, and give them the world. All of these notions seeded in vague aspiration and fertile emotion. They don't know what it is they want. But they know they want something. It is all too easily planted: this idea that we have what they want, and that we will share it with them.

The pandemonium which grips the city around them makes it that much easier for them to peel off, a splinter group weaving its way like mercury. And not as many as I'd thought. Twenty, maybe thirty of them. No bad thing. It will make it easier.

The building was once a furniture emporium. It is huge and sprawls round a junction, overlooking a roundabout. It has been empty for about a year now. The floors are still carpeted, that tough nylon shop-carpeting that was hard-wearing and could scorch the skin off the knees and elbows of children who took a tumble when chasing each other round the displays. There are patches that bear the outlines of the shapes of the stock that once decorated the place. Patches untrodden. Fresh. The exact opposite effect to lawn that has been covered and dies in the darkness.

These thoughts unbidden. Time ticking slowly.

I look out on the street below me. No sign of trouble down here yet. But the sound of sirens and the distant roar of rioting are certainly on the swell. I look out, anticipating them. They will be here soon.

Danny, Peter and John's mother are all here with me. *He* has promised to release her to my custody once the deed is done and the knife is in his hands. But I don't trust him. And I doubt he trusts me. Trust has long since left the party. Such is life. We all have our secrets.

Anna is waiting outside. She's been tasked with ensuring none of them leave once they're in. The building, for one night only, is to become an abattoir. That is the plan.

My flock tell me they are here.

From the window here on the second floor I see them sweep around the building opposite at a fair clip. They hurtle out and across the road, weaving without hesitation between the cars screeching and swerving to avoid them. Then I lose sight of them as they continue on round to the back of the emporium. I hear them then, jostling through the door at the back, in and up through the echoing chambers and deserted staircases of the store.

Anna counts them in, and once the last is confirmed Danny gives me a nod, and at that I call in my own.

Timing will now be everything. The next few moments will need executing with a delicacy and precision that daunts me. I have already watched one mob infestation mutate and spread like a plague – it doesn't take much – but if it happens again, in here, everything could go wrong. These next few minutes will be more dangerous than anything I've ever endeavoured to do in my long, long life. But it has to be done. It has to end.

The flock climb ominously up from the shadows below, less haste now, much more caution. The adrenaline that has fuelled their exodus to this place is now fizzling out. It won't be long before the cold whispers of disenchantment start firing them up again. They've been promised a leader. A purpose. An explanation. And they've been given an abandoned furniture outlet. It is up to me now to say some words.

I step out of the shadow and open my arms in welcome.

They stop, and spread out across the space before me, all eager to see who it is they have come to be enlightened by. The place is shadowy enough for my physical presence to maintain a sense of enigma. It is up to my words now to hold them in position long enough for my own flock to arrive and pen them in.

'Children...' I say.

I imagine that might inflame them. And it does.

'Who the fuck you calling children?' one of them asserts.

'When you have lived as long as I have, everyone is as a child. It is no bad thing. But I *have* lived a long time. What you all have been for days, perhaps weeks at most, I have been for centuries. I remember the last time this city burnt. And I remember *why*.'

They mutter among themselves, unsure whether my words are worth listening to or not. But that uncertainty is enough to hold them in place for now. They've nothing better to do.

'Why did it burn before?' one of the younger ones asks.

'Same reason it's burning this time. Because it deserved too. It needed to. You know, without forest fires, many forests would become overpopulated and choke. Cities are much the same. If not literal fire, then something similar will often do. Disease. Revolution. Genocide. Such things help keep the books balanced… ah… here you are.'

My flock softly enter the space and encircle *his* flock. His lot turn to face mine and they *bristle*. Quite the stand-off.

'Hush now, children. Understand this – we outnumber you. We are faster than you. We have been doing this longer than you. So what happens next is out of your hands. I have plans for you all. You may not like them, but you are still children and I'm afraid you have no say in the matter. Peter, Danny, I would prefer it if she sat this one out downstairs, if you don't mind?' I nod to John's mother.

Danny and Peter, consumed now with excitement at what is about to happen, nod enthusiastically. I smile quietly and look to one of mine. 'Take her downstairs.'

She is taken away.

And once she is gone, I get started.

CHAPTER TEN

ENTRAPMENT AND RELEASE

1

She is as good as her word. He. This so-called 'Rider'. Ridiculous name. *He* is as good as *his* word. No, she. It is still *her*, no matter the gender of her new hermitage. It is still her, inside the male rat-skin, keeping her promise. I hadn't been sure that she would. I had cause to mistrust her.

After centuries walking the earth at my side, just me and her against the world, she had decided to end things. And it was a relief. It was. She was right. I can't deny it. Looking back now, I can see an element of truth in her words. That it was I who despised the vermin that surrounded us. That swamped what little land there was left to roam. The night skies, which were the only skies we had left to us, they painted with light pollution, stealing away the stars from us. We would retreat into the lightless pockets, but we couldn't stay there indefinitely.

We had to eat.

And where there was food, there was filth. On the floor. In the sky. On the walls and in the water. There was no access to life without exposure to dirt. And it was all because of them. The rats. Swarming and overwhelming and overcoming every attack the planet's immune system would throw at them. What had begun as the equivalent of a global yeast infection had somehow mutated into a full-blown immunodeficiency syndrome. And the world started to die. Slowly, painfully. And the universe started to draw away from us. Casting us away like a sick runt. Because of *them*.

The rats.

And so what reason was there left to stay.

But she was right. I did all but get on and do it. I expressed every reason for not staying. I examined and observed and explained and challenged every new set of data. And every new set of data only strengthened my case.

There were moments of hope, that perhaps the tide might have turned. Eras when they would turn on each other and cut each other down in swathes, and I would pray that perhaps nature had found an antibody that beat their defences and would cause them to self-destruct. Cell suicide. But no. Every time, they would overcome and repopulate. Often they would boom.

There were plagues and outbreaks – influenzas and poxes – but nothing would touch them. They lived and wallowed and ate their own shit, abandoned their children and left their parents in boxes to rot, but still they marched on.

So. It is as it was. It was as it is. She was right.

I don't know why I needed her to go first. I didn't know I did. I just…

I don't know.

But now I am here. With Danny and Peter.

Dear, sweet Peter.

Perhaps if the world were a better place then there might have been hope for Peter. And perhaps if there were more like Peter there could have been hope for me. But too little, too late. What is done is done. I have no interest in staying any more. Too tired.

When first I discovered how she had deceived me, there was a moment when I wanted to destroy her. Devour her. And to carry on just to spite her. It is in my nature. And she knew that too. She knew everything.

That is in *her* nature.

But my anger and my hatred quickly dissipated. Peter was kind to me. Looked up to me. Trusted me. Danny less so. He never trusted me. But he cared for Peter. Looked out for him. He was good. Is good. Better than one might have expected. A shame for him too that things would end now as they had to end.

And the way things had to end was to be me, Danny and Peter back on the bench, rising with the morning sun. With the knife safely destroyed. And all of these other rat-children safely bled out, every last trace of me extinguished. And she could stay, if that is what she wants. I don't care any more. I just want to be done.

So I herd them in and send them out across the city to fetch the girl. It is a delicate operation as I am barely there within so many of them. Some of them I have entered directly, via the knife, and they hear me more clearly. A couple of them I have already brought across to us: those ones are on watch with her flock. They will more readily recognise the crows when they descend. But most of them I hardly haunt, passed on inadvertently by the first generation. These are the ones who needed a martyr to motivate them. And motivate them it has. And, having motivated them, I can move them round the obstacles between them and us. I am both shepherd and dog.

The rescue of the girl is fierce and curiously invigorating. It has been so long since I have hunted with a pack and it reminds me of a time when life was worth living. The speed and the power and the sheer kinetic release of it all. It *becomes* us. And it makes me stronger in them, which in turn engenders a germ of respect in them for me. It brings us closer.

It brings us closer. And reawakens something.

Something that has long been lost in me.

A lust.

As we then hurtle and glide through the streets towards our destiny, I remember what it felt like to chase through the trees and across the plains, hunting down monkeys before they became rats. I remember what it felt like to conjure motion from muscle, velocity from ideas. I remember the thump and rattle of running, the delight of air whipping past my skin, the roar of the world as it raced past me. I remember all of these things and I delight. As do these rat-children. They feel life as they've never felt it before. And they remind me of how it always used to feel. Before it slipped away. Before it had to mean something.

And when had that started? When had it started to require meaning, purpose? I can't even remember what it is that might have caused such a momentous shift. Such a catastrophic shift. When running and chasing and fighting and fucking and hurtling and pelting at full speed was surely the end in itself. What had I allowed myself to become? And why?

So perhaps now I am faltering. Could this be?

Could it be that perhaps I might like to stay for a while? Play for a while?

Could that be?

She would of course insist that I don't. That was the agreement.

But maybe the deal needs renegotiating.

Oh, we could get rid of most of them. I think I would keep Peter. Darling Peter. For a while at least. Danny and the woman could still burn. And then perhaps one of these ones. The fastest, the strongest. Yes… perhaps that is what I shall do.

It shouldn't be too hard to organise.

She doesn't even need to know.

She knows I only have the loosest control over them, spread as I am so thinly. Of course one of them could escape from the trap. It wouldn't be so unfeasible. They all want to survive, it wouldn't have to be my fault. It would in fact look very much the opposite. I would simply appear weak.

I consider taking one of them now. But to do so I would lose what little control I have over the rest. The cloud would break and *she* would know. And if she knew, I would never get the knife.

But then, do I even need the knife any more?

If I chose to stay, then what use the knife to me?

None.

But in her hands? She would for ever be able to seed me at will, sunder and spread me across the feral beasts, just to punish me and weaken me immeasurably.

No. It couldn't be left with her. I still need the knife.

So I bring them into the building as agreed.

I swarm up to the top floor as agreed and allow the trap to spring shut. She steps out of the shadows and says the one word that I know will make them buck and thrash against the loose grip I hold them in.

'Children…'

'Who the fuck you calling children?'

The one who asks that question is perhaps the one I shall keep. My frustration at her for poking at the hornet's nest is allayed by the help it has provided in making my decision. I allow myself now to move more into him – now that she has their attention, I need less to control the others. They will control themselves – *she* will control them – for the next few moments. They want to be here now. They want to hear what she has to say. They think they will get answers. It is what they will think until the moment they are devoured. And when that moment comes, I will be ready to move.

She is waffling on at them. Ever the drama queen. Some things never change. I miss what she says, but one of the rats I have brought in asks, 'Why did it burn before?'

'Same reason it's burning this time. Because it deserved too. It needed to. You know, without forest fires, many forests would become overpopulated and choke. Cities are much the same. If not literal fire, then something similar will often do. Disease. Revolution. Genocide. Such things help keep the books balanced… ah… here you are.'

Her flock softly enter the space and encircle my own rats. I feel my rats bristle and tense from afar, further afar now that I am in this one. This bold one.

'Hush now, children. Understand this – we outnumber you. We are faster than you. We have been doing this longer than you. So what happens next is out of your hands. I have plans for you all. You may not like them, but you are still children and I'm afraid you have no say in the matter. Peter, Danny, I would prefer it if she sat this one out downstairs, if you don't mind?'

Ah yes. Danny and Peter. I had almost forgotten them. Good that they are so well trained now. That I am entwined. I have them nod enthusiastically and go along with the script. Yes, take the rat-mother away. Let's just do this now.

I am excited beyond all compare.

I am on the cusp of a new life.

There are loose ends to be tied, for sure, but I have a lifetime in which to tie them.

And then the script changes.

'You might all have felt something inside you that should not have been there. An ugly spirit. A virus that whispers in your ear and talks to you as the world talks to you. It probably calls you *rat*.'

No.

What is she doing?

I step forward and cry out, 'What are you doing?'

Downstairs, Peter, Danny and Anna are seized.

The rats look around nervously.

'Take that one.' She – *he* – points me out to her flock, the me that I had silently moved my focus into, the me that spoke out when she altered the plan. I make a break for it, but they are too fast. They seize me. I buck and writhe and snap my teeth at them.

'What are you doing, bitch? What are you doing?!'

She looks at them then, and speaks softly, reassuringly, 'But children: I think I can help. I think I might have a cure for you. You will always bear the mark, but I believe I can rid you of *him*.'

She looks at me as she spits that final word.

Then she takes from her pocket the knife.

She clicks it two notches out of its handle, tilts her head and looks me square in the eye, ''Til death us do part, my love. 'Til death…'

My mouth is dry. No words form there.

What is she doing?

Then she plunges the knife into her arm.

2

This is the first time I have ever done it this way around. It is as new to me as it was for all of them. But it is not anything other than I had expected. There is the initial roar as he rages into me, swiftly followed by the disparate ebb back into him. Disparate because there is no him to ebb into – only them, all of them – and a good thing too, as he would have devoured me.

And I become theirs, his. Their child. His child.

And they my parents. In a way.

It is, in its own manner, somehow beautiful. Not unlike, I can only imagine, being born.

It hurts. But it is wonderful.

I fly into them and ride a wave of all of their lives. A river of dreams and experiences, connected through him, and now also by me. Intertwined and tangled. The imaginings of their childhood dreams blended with the brutal realities of their cold, largely neglected lives. They still remember the taste of running and jumping and tumbling and laughing. It is still there. But it is melting away.

Poor babies.

And there *he* is, scheming away behind the rows. Plotting his new life. As I'd known he would. It had been inevitable. He barely remembers the last time he had to kick the habit, his addiction to them. The writhing nightmares and tortu-ous pangs of hunger. He'd had to give them up, not because he hated them, not because they were rats, but because he liked it too much. He had been losing himself in them. They kept becoming more and more and more. Their ideas and intentions grow ever more distant from the simple urges and drives that he was born to. They became harder for him to understand, and the more they moved away from him the more he wanted to be them. The less able he was to resist them. The more lost in them he became.

So he had to give them up. They were destroying him.

And he had. He'd given them up. And from that moment forth he'd started to hate them. And not just them, everything. Life itself. And so of course he would succumb, given the faintest sniff. Of course he would wilt and go back to his old ways. Of course he would renege on what had been agreed and elect to cling on. To him, life was a cheap high. Because he could take it or leave it. And so he had. But it *was* a high. And so he would take it. It was inevitable.

If I were to allow him.

I will not allow him.

His time is done.

It would be easier to have seen the plan through his way and to have simply devoured this so-called horde, Peter, Danny and Anna included. That would see to him. But I will not sacrifice them for him. They are worth too much. They are worth everything. I will not be like him. No matter what. So, this won't be easy. But it is the only way.

I have told mine what to do if it goes wrong.

If it goes wrong I depart with him and they carry on without me.

They will be fine.

And so the knife goes into me and it might as well be his teeth. Whatever absurd alchemy has etched him into the cheap steel of the knife, it binds us, as has always been the way. Our double-helixed selves smashed into each other and hard-wired together. So, after the initial infective surge I'm pulled out of myself and into him, into them. There then follows the infinite birthing moment that charts the long arc over the top of the parabola of time and space before I must pull back into myself, bringing him with me.

In that moment he charges at me and pounces. Top predator, hungry, ready to devour his prey. If he feeds on me in here, I will become his. And that will be it. And that too is as it has always been. Some things are just made a certain way. But I am of course ready. No one has more experience of being that top predator than I do. In here, in the deadlights, I skip to the side and feel the full weight of him land in the anti-space beside me. He growls. And he summons himself, all of himself, drawing nearly his entirety in now from the children. He quickens and turns and prowls in again towards me. He is the true beast that he has become over centuries of progressive dehumanisation. He snaps at me, the fangs in his oversized jaws throwing notions of saliva and rage.

'Come on then, rat-lover. You chose to enter here: what are you waiting for? Submit.'

'Where is it that you think you are?' I ask him.

He snarls again and lets the growl rumble on before lifting it at the end into a roar. 'No more games. I'm in you. I saw you put me into you.'

I dance off to the side of him, silently. He stalks on, unaware that I have moved. I can sense him prowling the darkness of the arc. It is all sense and suggestion. There is no real body or tangible identity out here on the arc. Just these selves, ghosts and rumours streaking through the nowhere. So any teeth or claws or hunched angry shoulders, any sylph-like grace or mercurial prowess – it's all projection, metaphor, allegory. It's all a dance. And it should be his dance to lead. I'm breaking all the rules, and it is driving him mad. Needling his ugly spirit, forcing him to pull every last filament of it back in from the children until he is whole again, and is in here. Then it is time.

'You are a fool. You are on the arc. There is no *you* out here. No *me*. There is just the arc. How can you still not know that?'

He swivels and leaps but he is slow, and I leap first and I grab him and I sink the notion of teeth into him. I sink into him and lock my jaws and cling on to his bucking and writhing body and the moment passes. The dance ends. And we slide down the other side of the arc.

Everything accelerates then, the frozen children standing there in the darkness looking at me, youthful terror in their eyes. Some of them are crying. They too have experienced everything that has just happened, as witnesses. It happened within them. And it was terrifying. More terrifying than anything they have endured so far. They were as babes being fought over by toothsome monsters, both of whom want to eat them whole. We are the horrors from the stories their parents never told them.

My, what large teeth we have.

They look at me and they are quiet. Mine look at me too. They haven't shared the moment as the others did, but they have an idea of what must have just taken place. I had talked them through what I had planned.

I pull the knife from my arm and drop it to the floor.

One of mine starts forward to pick it up.

'No!' I hiss. 'Don't touch it. Nobody touch it. And all of you stay back. It is not done yet.'

Because there is still work to do. I have freed them. But he is still in the room.

I feel the backs of my legs tighten and a prickle runs up from my arm, once round my chest and then charges up into my jaw. My throat starts to tighten. And his voice thunders around my skull, 'Time to die.'

The children see me stiffen and once again start towards me, and once again I hiss them back. I close my eyes then and turn away from them and back into myself. And I run. Into the corridors, and away from him. It is as it was when I was searching for this sanctuary I now live in – entering into their prone bodies at the clinic, I'd find them deserted, and I would walk the empty hallways. They would bend and rearrange, but they were navigable. Not like the deadlights of the arc. Out there on the arc was nothing but ephemeral notion. In here everything was a soft bio-form reality. Malleable and evolving. But solid. And ordered, in its way. I knew my way around. And I knew where I needed to take him.

And thankfully, inevitably, he gave chase. That was the final gamble. That I would turn and run and that he would stay and take control. But, somewhere back there, I felt my body go limp and fall to the ground. And I could hear him chasing after me. His fury was now its own master, and he its slave. He had lost all control. He wanted nothing now other than to capture me and destroy me. But I had things to show him. Things he needed to know. Truths I had to help him understand. It was the only way now. The die was cast.

And so at last it comes to this.
For such is love sometimes.
And such is life.
And so it goes.
So it goes.

CHAPTER ELEVEN

ASCENSION AND DENIAL

1

We tumble from the twisted tunnels of her mind and out into an ancient woodland. The trees are thick-trunked and stand some distance apart from each other. They are old trees. Oak. The ground beneath their branches springy. Alive. I falter then. Of course I do.

What new trick is this?

She is waiting for me. She looks as she did back then. When she first took me.

She looks beautiful.

She takes my breath away and with it goes everything else: the rage, the murderous intent, the hatred. I can't believe it. But it is true.

And I remember then which of us was first, and who belongs to whom. That I am hers.

I have always been hers.

She holds out her hand to me and smiles, 'Come on.'

I hesitate. This can't be possible. I raise my hands before my eyes, turning them over for inspection. They are young. They are human. They are as they were. I shake my head. I can feel tears welling. It can't be possible.

The air is crisp, and there is the finest carpeting of ground mist. The world is quiet. The occasional hooting of a distant, sleepy-sounding owl. I break out in goose-bumps and a shiver ricochets through me. My breath plumes in front of my face.

My breath! It has been an eternity since I have breathed. And yet now, here it is. I breathe deep, and it is as if I have been thirsty for a lifetime and never realised. The air in my lungs, oxygenating my blood, is exquisite. The tears do come then. I do nothing to hold them back.

I look at her, through my tears, and see that she is crying too. She still has her hand outstretched to me. She nods. I whisper three words, a question to which I already know the answer, 'Where are we?'

'Home.'

'How?'

'Does it matter?'

And now, after everything that's gone before, I suppose it doesn't matter. It doesn't matter and I don't care. However she has done it, and however hard I have fought her, it's all OK. I go to her and take her hand. She pulls me to her and holds me then. Holds me tight. Then she pulls back and, holding my hand, leads me away through the trees.

I follow willingly. I know where we are going. And I want to go there.

The walk feels like it takes for ever. But it doesn't. The fattening moon hanging high in the sky, barely flickering through the leafy canopy, drops hardly at all in the time it takes us to reach our final destination. And yet I savour so much with every step. The taste of the air, the chill feel of it. The brightness of the stars in the sky through the gaps in the trees. The sound of the breeze whispering softly through the branches. The occasional scurry of tiny and terrified wildlife that breaks into a run at our approach. All of these things as they should be. All of these things as they were before. Before the people changed and became the vermin that would tear it all down, concrete it over and purge the stars from the heavens.

We come to the place and we stop. She puts her hand on my chest and has me wait in the treeline. Someone approaches from the settlement. He is young, athletic-looking. He is wearing the skins and leathers that are all that there is to wear in this place, this time. He walks out to meet us. He stops a few lengths distant and tilts his head to look at us. The passing cloud that has held him in shadow moves on across the sky, and the moonlight reveals him.

And he is me.

My heart leaps into my throat.

Mesmerised.

He looks at her and nods.

She lets go of my hand and steps back into the shade.

And then I am him, looking back into the trees. I can't see her, but I know she is there. I can sense her. And this is how it was. This is how it happened. I can sense her, and most of me wants her. I can almost taste her. The wildness of her. The infinite otherness. I tilt my head and squint my eyes and smile. I open my heart and my mind to her and show her how different I am to the others at my back in their nests. I transmit my longing to run with her.

But then a soft, quiet voice inside me whispers against this youthful hunger. It dares to suggest that perhaps, just perhaps, I *do* belong here. That I am of the nest. And that the nest needs my dreams, more perhaps than she does. Perhaps she doesn't need them at all. Perhaps she just *wants* them. Lusts for them, even.

She doesn't step out into plain sight. And this time, unlike last time, I don't go to her.

I turn my back on her and walk back to my people.

I walk back and I lie down, and when I awake the sun is in the sky and it doesn't burn me. It is warm, and the world is so vibrant and full of colour and awash with sound – chatter and laughter, the clatter of labour, all of these things that I'd dreamt in the night had slipped away from me. When I'd dreamt that I'd become a monster that journeyed to a place from which I couldn't return, and which made no sense to me. Where the children of my children, on and on, beyond I don't know how many countless generations, had turned into things I didn't understand and of which I could no longer be a part. And which I'd spent so much energy loathing for wanting to take the world into their own hands, as I have taken this world into mine. Loathing them for taking the world from me but not caring for it as I do. For doing things their way. And I had worn them down. Convinced them they were worthless because they weren't like me. And in holding on, I'd taken the fire from their eyes, and they'd become lost in the darkness, and turned in on themselves.

What a dream. Such sadness.

But I am awake now.

Thank the gods I am awake.

I push myself up and walk out into my life, and the life I'd dreamt in the night falls away from me. As does the hunger and the disdain. I run with my brothers and find food; we engineer new methods of construction that strengthen our shelters and make them warmer; we discover new means of storing our foods for the cold winter months. And slowly we progress.

I take a wife. And we live a life together and it is good. Our children are strong, and we are blessed in that most of them survive the pup stage. The ones that we lose bring a sadness that doesn't pass, but it is a sadness that gilds the joy of the ones that live. It gives that joy substance, texture. It is a substance and texture that I frequently curse and wish away, but often too it enfolds me and adds worth to what I still have. And I grow old with her, and my children mature into adulthood and they take the world from my hands. And they manage it differently than I had. But it is theirs to manage now. Not mine. I am too old. My work is done now that they are upright.

I walk with her, my wife, most days in among the trees. Sometimes a memory fleets by, a memory of a dream I once had as a young buck, and it leaves a strange pang – as if I had seen too much, more than was natural. And that seeing all too often precludes knowing.

In seeing and living too much we become lost. It is the way of it.

I am starting to feel a little lost now. In my dotage, with my wife, walking through the trees. Our children now own the world, some of them are starting to have children of their own. And some of those children, they look at us as I looked at the parents of my parents back when I was a buck. Back when I thought I was better than them. Back when I had a choice to make, at the treeline. A choice I can no longer remember, that is as a dream. But I had thought myself better than those tired old husks that so disdained me and my youthful ways. But they passed on and the world fell into our hands and we had to bear it. And we did. Until our bodies wearied and we could bear it no longer, and we handed it on. We handed it on and then told the children how to do it.

That they were doing it wrong.

I laugh at that and my wife looks at me.

I shake my head.

It is in our nature, I guess, to not trust our children. To believe they will drop the world and break it. Perhaps it is for the best that we depart it when we do, or they might start believing us. And in believing us they would surely drop it.

We live out our days and they are good. She leaves before me. And that is a greater sadness for me than the pups we lost. Greater, and better. The sadness of losing her is also a promise. A promise that I can leave too. That I don't have to stay. Not that I have to leave because the world is rotting, but because the world simply doesn't need me any more. That my work here is done. And everything is OK.

At last, everything is OK.

One night I awaken. The wind is soft and somewhere distant an owl is hooting half-heartedly. I push myself up and out from beneath my shelter. I pull on an extra skin – the night is cold – and I head out into the moonlit darkness, not so dark at all. I take the stick that helps me stand now and I totter away from the settlement, down towards the treeline.

Something is waiting for me.

Someone.

I stop a few lengths distant from them and tilt my head. My eyes aren't what they once were and I can't make them out. When they step forward, my heart leaps into my throat. It is her. And with her a young one, a buck, gimlet eyes looking at me with as much shock as I'm sure I am reflecting back. For he is me. As I was. As somewhere within I've no doubt I will always be.

And then I am him, beside her once again, and I am watching the young me turning away from us and moving back up the slope to the settlement. Back to the life that is his.

I lean on my stick and exhale. I am tired now.

She reaches out and puts her hand on mine. The tiredness in my bones takes on an unearthly weight then, and there starts a skittering behind my ribcage that reminds me of a small, injured bird I once found on the ground. That had died in my hands as I cradled it.

It is my time.

She helps me to the ground and props me up against the trunk of the tree. She strokes my cheek and she weeps. Such sadness, these young ones. I smile at her, and say for her not to worry. That this is the way of things. That this is as it should be. That my work is long since done and all I could achieve by staying is undoing it. I don't want to poison my children. Or their children. I have to let go.

She smiles so sadly then. 'You are beautiful…' she whispers then, 'I love you. I always have. And I always will. And I'm so sorry…'

I shake my head wearily at her and tell her to hush.

Behind her the sky is turning red. A new day is dawning.

I look to the east and wait for *her*. She that reddens the sky in anticipation of her arrival. She that chases away the night.

She leans in and kisses me, softly, lingeringly, on my lips, and once again she takes my breath away. Then she slips away back into the shadow of the trees and leaves me there, breathless and done. My chest is still, but my eyes and my mind hold on for those last few moments, so that I can see her, the sun, one last time.

And then, there she is.

Rising majestic over the hill and the settlement that sits atop it.

She rises, she that gives life and taketh it away.

She rises and I look into her.

She rises, and I rise with her.

2

By the time the man with the scar across his face opens his eyes, all of the others in the room are calm enough, but deeply concerned. Those that had hosted the old-one know that he is gone now. They know that the man on the floor took him away from them. But they're not sure how whatever has just happened will have affected him. He lies there for a moment and looks up at the ceiling.

One of the flock that he'd brought with him steps forward.

She has been one of his flock for a few years now, ever since he'd saved her from the group of drunks that had set upon her. She'd been living in a box at the time. Story of her life. He'd pulled her out of harm's way and snapped a few drunken limbs and taken her back to the farm. He'd nursed her back to health and invited her to stay. To help with the running of the place. In time she'd asked for the gift. She'd wanted to help people the way he'd helped her. She didn't feel cut out for farm work. She felt that *outreach* work would be a better fit. And outreach required the gift. That was how it worked.

So, over those few years, they had slowly grown as a group, as a *family*, but they all understood the need for absolute secrecy. That the farm was for him, in effect, a secure retreat from a violent relationship. His own woman's retreat. She teased him about that from time to time, kindly, and he would smile. He would smile and say, 'Soon... soon...', and his eyes would flit away as if somewhere else he was being watched and his secret might get out.

It would always be soon. Always on the horizon. She didn't think he would ever leave the old-one. People never did. Not when they'd stuck it out that long. Once they'd made it that far they always seemed to get locked in it until the bitter end. And the end would always be truly bitter. No matter what. It was almost a badge of honour.

But then one day he told them it was time. She didn't know what had happened to push him to the decision. But something in his eyes had shifted. Something in his posture. He stood slightly straighter. Like he wasn't carrying anything any more.

That had been just over a month ago now. It hadn't gone smoothly. It had been a terrifying time for all of them. They'd thought they might lose him. And they'd not been at all sure about the boy, John, whom he'd brought back with him. The boy had been mean. Still was pretty mean. Might yet still grow up to be mean. But the man had treated him fairly and the boy had responded positively. Enough. So far. He'd played his part in putting things right, and he'd not allowed his petulance to run away with him such that he's upended any plans. He'd not given them away. That had been her greatest concern. And he'd not asked for the gift. Which had also been a relief. She'd assumed he would, but he hadn't. It seemed his better nature was better than hers. That he had less need to vent. Less need to bare his teeth. Perhaps in time he'd change his mind. Perhaps he was a better person than she gave him credit for.

She steps forward and looks down on the prone, dazed figure on the floor. His eyes roll lazily across to look at her. She asks him, 'What's the word?'

She needs to know he's still who he was. That he isn't the other one.

The man on the floor smiles up at her.

'Grease. Grease is the word.'

She smiles. He smiles.

'Good,' she says, reaching down to take his hand and pull him to his feet. 'Is it done?'

His smile fades somewhat. He nods. He says nothing. Then he steps round her and looks down at the knife. It is where he'd thrown it after he'd pulled it from his arm. It is glowing red. Getting redder. He steps back from it, over towards the young crowd watching him carefully. The light coming through the sole unboarded window is brightening.

'We need to move. We need to be quick. We need to be careful – stay away from trouble. Especially you lot...' He looks at the hooded flock that sparked the chaos engulfing the streets. 'They'll be looking for you. And if they take you in, we won't be coming for you. We do things differently. Understand?'

They nod solemnly, respectfully, and then start off down the stairs. He is the last to follow. He glances back at the knife. It is now glowing white, like a light bulb. As if it is falling into the sun.

Somewhere, a part of it is.

A drop of molten metal falls to the floor from its tip and a small flame plumes into existence. He can almost feel the warmth being given off by the steel from here, some metres distant. He turns and heads down to the next floor.

They are waiting for him. But not just the flock.

Danny is here. He looks at the scarred man with dispassionate eyes. He is tired, and he is angry. But he has reconciled himself to his situation. He won't miss the old-one. He felt nothing for him. 'What happens to the boy who did this to me?' he asks.

The scarred man looks at him and gives him an honest response. 'He moves on. You should do the same.' Danny nods and frowns at the same time. It was the answer he'd expected. But not the one he'd wanted.

Peter is wailing. He is in Anna's arms and sobbing like the young child he still is. Was. Will for a long time continue to be. He refuses to look at the scarred man, or his flock. He hates them. They have taken away the only person who has ever cared for him. The only person who ever protected him, stood up for him, made him feel safe. He doesn't feel safe any more. He is scared and he is crying. He clings to Anna. She holds him tight and shushes him. He snuffles and sobs into the crook of her neck. She looks across at the scarred man and locks eyes with him. They see each other. The faintest flicker of a smile on her lips. Then a nod.

He nods back and understands her smile. She is one of them now. She is with them. Her sympathies for the old-one hadn't extended to sympathy for his ways. She had come to pity him. She didn't think she would miss him.

And then John's mother is also here, cowed and terrified. Wide-eyed and docile. She doesn't know where to be, where to look, what to do. The scarred man goes to her, puts a finger under her chin and raises her face to look at him. Her eyes are awash with tears and she is shaking. He tells her that she has nothing to fear. She will not be harmed. That they will now take her to her son.

Her face folds and creases and weeps. She puts her hands to her face and he holds her.

A crackling from upstairs gets them moving. A hole burns through the ceiling above their heads and the knife, molten now, pours through. It is too bright to look at. It is the heart of a star. The heat it throws off is incredible. Impossible. They move then.

Down, out into the streets. They break into small groups, each smaller group led by one of the scarred man's flock, and they make flight to somewhere safe, a place in the city, not too far from the now blazing emporium. A place where they can hide from the sun, before heading back to their home beyond the concrete and the crowds.

At the safe place the scarred man counts them in.

All of them.

All except one.

3

Picking through the smouldering rubble of the building, the fire crews found no human remains. At least there was that. Not that there was any guarantee that they wouldn't yet. But so far, so not so bad. Having said that, what they did find suggested the kind of heat that wouldn't leave remains. Just ash. Incineration.

Tom paced the perimeter demarcated by the police tape some fifty metres distant and felt adrift. The last month and a bit of his life had seemed like some ever-intensifying fugue. What started as just plain weird at the park bench had evolved to something more sinister back at the same bench a week later, before then blossoming through full-blown horror at the flat into a situation approximating an actual nightmare from there on in – Anna's mysterious disappearance, the further murders, the missing children and young adults, the shooting fuck-up, the assault on the police station and now this: the city in flames, with others across the country fast going the same way.

It was madness. And it shook him to his core.

His foundational belief that the world, humanity, whatever, was on a gradual curve up and away from the fanged bloodlust from whence we came didn't stack up so neatly in the wake of these last few weeks' events. He wondered this morning if perhaps Anna hadn't had a point after all.

What was it Anna had said to him that night in the café? *You'd be surprised what children can do these days, Tom.*

That was it. That's what she'd said.

He wasn't so sure that he would be surprised. Not any more. Not today. Not after the night the city had just lived through.

She'd been right, after all, it seemed.

A part of him blamed her. Blamed Anna. He knew it didn't make sense, but he had to acknowledge it. He did. This part of his mind blamed her for saying it out loud and making it so. Her, and people like her, assuming the world was gone to shit, their quiet cynicism slowly polluting the world until… well, until lo, so it came to pass. He shook his head at himself. He knew this was bigger than that. And somewhere, deep down, he believed that nothing much had really changed. Less than a hundred years ago the industrialised slaughter of entire races was still very much the fashion and this was nothing like that. This was just a squall. A particularly vicious storm. But it would pass. It didn't herald the dawn of the descent of man.

He hoped. He hoped. He continued to hope.

He nursed a coffee in a takeout cup and looked up through the charred and smouldering walls and glassless windows of the old furniture emporium. He remembered this place from when he was little. He'd come here with his parents. They'd bought bunk-beds for him and his brother, their firstborn. His parents still had them, the bunks. His nephews slept on them now when they stayed with their grandparents. His own daughter probably would too when she was a bit older and started going for sleepovers. He remembered the day his folks had driven in from the suburbs to choose them, spending the afternoon chasing through the fake bedrooms parked up next to mocked-up living rooms and home offices. It had reminded him of a book they had in the school library that had pictures of buildings with the walls removed so you could see what was inside. Little arrows pointing to things named in English and French. He'd loved that book. And he'd loved this furniture shop. But it was gone now.

But then it had been gone for a while already. Emptied and abandoned. A husk. Now, however, it had been cremated and it would never be back. No matter how hard he wished it. And he only wished it at all because he was sat here looking at its blackened shell.

He hadn't thought of it for years.

But that's how life worked. You might happily forget something only to remember it once it was gone. And only then would you miss it. When it was too late. The most tired cliché in the world. But still true. Just like all the other clichés. He wondered what would be next. What was he neglecting to remember right now as he sat there pining over the loss of a store that he'd not thought of since childhood?

He missed childhood.

And he felt sad.

A deep, aching sadness. And he worried that this time he wouldn't be able to shake it.

He swilled his nearly empty cup and slugged down the last mouthful. Grimaced. Headed across the street to find a bin. He wasn't sure what else he was going to achieve here. Especially in the wake of so much else going on all over the place. The brutal attack on the police station that had sparked the subsequent bedlam had been carried out by a nondescript gang of hooded youths. Witnesses had falteringly described a peculiarly menacing air they had about them, which, coupled with their seemingly inhuman brutality – how matter-of-factly they attacked and murdered so many trained police officers, outside and inside the station – painted a picture somehow beyond conceit. They'd freed the girl and gone, swept away in a landslide of directionless, inflammatory destruction. But then it did all provide a dreadful, impossible continuity to the wave of crimes they'd been investigating over the previous weeks.

Survivors had made all sorts of wild statements about what had happened and none of it made any sense. They described things that weren't possible. Kids moving so fast they were a blur. Throats being ripped out with bare hands. Officers being thrown across rooms. Doors torn from hinges. Hysterical, outlandish, unbelievable, impossible. So why then did he believe it?

It was something about the words the desk clerk quoted the ringleader as saying to him: 'We're here for the girl, rat.' It niggled at his mind. It was such a small, insignificant detail in a spuming ocean of the stuff, and yet his mind hollered that there was something to it. That there was a connection to be made.

But he hadn't been able to make it. Too tired. Too much else to try and absorb.

He'd come here when he heard the description of the crowd of kids that had swarmed across the street in the direction of the building not half an hour before the first reports of smoke. He didn't know if he was the first to make a connection, or if he was in fact just the first to be losing the plot and seeing connections where there were none to be made. Perhaps it was just that when he imagined a swarm of hooded kids moving as one in a blur through a police station, and a similar swarm sweeping through busy, moving traffic as one, in a blur, he imagined the same kids. So it was tenuous.

At best. Because all the statements were clearly tinted by the exaggerating lens of panic, and none of them withstood any sort of serious scrutiny. But still. He was begging and not choosing. There wasn't much else to go on. Or rather, there was so much else to go on it didn't really make a fat lot of difference where he started.

He dropped the cup in the bin and stuffed his hands in his pockets.

He wished Anna was here. As much as she could drive him mad, and as little as he shared her world view, she was always good for perspective. She could always look in on things from the other side, and quite frequently it was this very stereoscopy of their vision as a team that would illustrate the nature of the crime. Without her he felt like he was walking around with a patch over one eye – and that he was misjudging everything. His perspective was all out of whack. But, she wasn't here. Hadn't been for a while. Not since she'd gone wrong that night and walked out of his life.

He started to head across to his car.

He thought back to that evening. The evening everything had tilted over the edge into the realm of the absurd. The horror-show in the flat. The missing teeth.

Fuck. The missing teeth. He'd forgotten about that.

No wonder she'd felt funny.

Her last words to him: *I feel funny*.

Her last words before getting up and leaving.

Her last words, a curious final little flourish to conclude her final, brutal assessment of the situation: *I'll tell you who stabbed Danny, Tom. Children did it. Filthy little rat-children. You'll see. But you'll never understand. You're too soft.*

He took two more steps and then froze. His blood ran cold.

Filthy little rat-children.

His eyes widened.

We're here for the girl, rat.

He stood there in the shadow of the burnt emporium and looked around for something solid. Something, anything that would tell him his mind had flipped and was seeing patterns that simply weren't there. Couldn't be there. Something, anything that would reassure him.

But everywhere he looked he saw faces riven with confusion and fear. He saw smoke and broken buildings. He saw police tape and aftermath. Everything was falling apart and nothing was in its place or as it should be, and if he was seeing patterns it might be because he was tired, or it might be because he was coming apart at the seams, or it might be because there were patterns.

We're here for the girl, rat.

Filthy little rat-children.

He got himself moving then, got into the car and put the key in the ignition.

This all started going supernova back at that flat. And they'd been at the flat because of the burnings on the bench. And here he was again at another burn, with nothing left but ash. And the only other person in the world who had joined any of these dots with him had disappeared in the immediate wake of it all ramping up.

She knew something.

She had to know something.

She was the only connective tissue in this whole sorry mess.

Filthy little rat-children.

Fuck.

Children had been disappearing.

Filthy little rat-children.

He turned the key in the ignition, put the car into gear and sped away.

4

She ignores the knocking on the door until it becomes a little frantic. She doesn't sigh or grumble or express any kind of irritation or frustration that someone is dragging her from her bed at this hour because she doesn't feel these things. She doesn't feel anything. Not any more. She goes to the door simply because it's the surest way to make the tapping stop.

She rubs her eyes and pushes the pile of letters on the doormat to one side, reaches to unhook the chain and finds it already dangling. Careless. She doesn't care. She turns the oval knob on the lock and pulls the door half open.

What she sees outside is not possible.

Her heart stops while her brain desperately tries to fire up and assess the ridiculous information it is receiving and deliver an assessment on its feasibility. The sky beyond the balcony is starting to brighten. A clear, bright winter's day is on its way. The sun will soon be up. And there on the stoop, pushing himself into the shade of the corner, still wearing the school uniform he'd been wearing the last time she saw him over a month ago now on the morning of the day he died, is her son.

She freezes, and in that frozen moment tumbles slowly, wordlessly back into her life.

Her heart continues to hold.

Her mouth falls open and silence comes out.

He looks up at her with fear in his pale eyes, fear and something else. Something like age. Oldness. He looks haunted. Like he's lived the entirety of another life since he's been gone. He looks at her and says just one word: 'Mummy?'

That starts her heart again. It thunders and clatters and blood rushes to her head. She wobbles on her feet and her vision narrows down to a tunnel. She almost blacks out and goes down, but doesn't – she leans against the door frame and takes a deep breath while at the same time frantically shoving the door open against the letter-drift fighting against her on the floor behind it.

She falls to her knees and puts her hands on his face and touches him tentatively to confirm he is real.

He is cold. Freezing.

But he is very real. Very there.

He looks tiredly at her face while her hands flit and fret across his whole body before flying around behind him and pulling him into a crushing embrace. She makes a strange sound then, as she holds him, something between a guttural moan and a warbling sing-song trill. He allows her to sweep him into her embrace, falling into her bosom, his knees bending and giving up his weight to her. He rests his head on her shoulder and closes his eyes. 'Mummy,' he whispers.

'Oh baby. Oh, my baby boy…'

'Mummy… can we go inside?'

She doesn't answer him. She takes it as an instruction as opposed to a request and simply goes back into the flat, carries him through to the now litter-strewn living room. She puts him on the sofa and sits beside him and tries to devour him with her eyes. A part of her mind tells her with no hint of doubt in its voice that she has now crossed the line from grief to insanity. The rest of her mind doesn't care. The rest of her mind welcomes insanity as a perfectly acceptable alternative to the endless agony of her loss. And here insanity is, sitting on the sofa beside her, looking weary beyond description, pale and cold. But it *is* him. And he *is* looking at her. And there *is* love in his eyes.

The rising sun starts to snoop around the upper corners of the room. He looks up at the band of light and then sadly down at his hands. 'Could you close the curtains?'

She does so without hesitation. She clicks the light on as she returns to him. 'Where have you been, baby? Where have you *been*?'

'I've been away, Mama. I can't say, really. It's hard to explain. But I'm back now. Is that OK? Is it OK for me to come back? Can I stay?' His blue eyes widen and well up and his bottom lip starts to tremble. He starts to shake and can barely look at his mother. That is when she breaks. Again.

Breaks from a million tiny pieces back into one. When she becomes a mother again.

She pulls him to her again, holds him again, and tells him of course. Of course he can stay. She never wants to be away from him ever again. And if he ever puts a scare on her like that again she'll probably kill him herself. She rocks him back and forth and he sobs into her breast for some time, and after a while he falls asleep on her. He doesn't snore.

Because he doesn't breathe.

She shakes him when she notices that, her heart ready once more to drop her directly back into the dread embrace of the nightmare. She shakes him and he murmurs, and his eyes flutter reluctantly open. 'Mama?'

'Baby... why don't you breathe? Why aren't you breathing?' There is a shrill splinter in her voice.

'Because I died, Mama. Someone killed me. But then this old thing brought me back, and he's been keeping me all this time. I wanted to come home, Mama, I swear it. But he wouldn't let me. He made me stay. He hated everything. He made me do things...'

She pales at that, and swallows. 'What did he make you do?'

'He just... he just got inside my head and... he... I was like a robot for him. He was in my head and he made the decisions and... he just made me do the stuff that he had to get done for him because he didn't have a body of his own any more and he couldn't do anything without me. I don't want to talk about it Mama. He brought me back though. And now he's gone. So it's OK, Mama.' His voice rises into a wail and his face wrenches into the bawl of a child whose sadness is too large to contain. 'It's OK Mama…' he sobs.

She doesn't understand a word of it. It makes no sense whatsoever. Sleep-talk, surely. She holds him close and he cries and he cries and eventually he goes back to sleep.

This time she doesn't wake him.

He sleeps the whole day. She checks him regularly, and each time she does so she gently pokes or nudges him to check for a response. Her son doesn't breathe any more and that terrifies her. But he wriggles and turns away from her when she pokes him, and that is enough to put her mind at rest. Enough for now.

She has her boy back. He is different now. But he is still him. Still her Danny. And that is enough. They'd figure everything else out as they go.

He wakes up to the smell of frying onions and the sound of boiling water bubbling on the stove. Bolognaise. The flat has been tidied and it feels like home again. He pushes himself up and goes through to the kitchen. She is humming to herself as she cooks. He looks at her with tired eyes. 'Mama?'

She turns and smiles at him.

'I'm gonna get my 'jamas on. And have a wash. OK?'

'OK sweetie. I'm cooking your favourite.' She grins and there is joy in her eyes.

'I know, Mama. I'm not… not too hungry though.' Not for what she is preparing. He'll have to talk to her about that too. But not yet.

Not yet.

Some of the joy leaves her eyes at that, not all of it, but some. 'Maybe I'll have some later. I'm just tired and wanna get in my 'jamas. You have some now though.' He nods enthusiastically at her. 'And maybe we can watch a film?'

He goes then and washes and changes and tries to pretend that everything can return to normal. He knows that it can't. He isn't the same as before. Nor is she. But maybe just for a little while, everything can be the same as it was.

Maybe they can pretend.

When he goes back through to the living room, the lights are dim and the movie cued up. A plate with the remnants of pasta sauce painted across it sits on the coffee table in front of her. He parks himself on the sofa beside her and snuggles up. She folds her arm round him and takes his cold hand in hers. She hits play and the movie starts.

The movie has werewolves in it.

His friends told him so.

He likes werewolves.

They watch the movie together.

She squeezes his hand and he squeezes hers back.

At some point a tear weaves silently across her cheek.

They move into an uncertain future together. For the moment it is OK.

For the moment.

And he doesn't offer her the gift. And nor does she ask for it. Not yet.

Not yet.

EPILOGUE

GLORY

1

Tom stood on the bridge and watched the sun go down over the water. The land was flat and uncrowded here. He liked it here. It was everything the city wasn't.

The air was cold. Winter had stormed in after a mild – hot in places – autumn and the chill really bit. He pulled up the collar of his heavy wool coat, turned south and walked along the road towards The White Hart. He went in and ordered a pint of the local ale and found himself a seat beside the fire. He undid the buttons of his coat but kept it on. He leant back in his seat and looked at the fire through the drink. A harmony of gold.

It had been a year since everything. Since the city collectively, and momentarily, lost its mind and tore itself apart. A year since the world had found a million other things to fret about and it had all slipped without fanfare into the past.

And a year since Anna had disappeared.

He raised the drink to his lips and took a sip. It was good. It always was. He took another and set it back down. One pint before the three-mile walk along the riverside track back to the cottage, where his wife and daughter would be waiting for him. Dinner would be ready in an hour. Plenty of time. He needn't hurry. Within reason.

They'd been coming here for years, but on this occasion it was more than it had ever been before. It had always been restorative, but this time it was deeper, richer. Better. It felt better.

He felt better.

He'd found nothing at Anna's flat when he'd got there. He'd kicked the door open and gone straight in. She hadn't been there. There was no sign that she'd been there recently. No sign that she hadn't. There'd been no note. No voicemail on her phone. Except for a couple of automated insurance sales calls. Nothing. Except for all her stuff. Her whole life. Still there. Untouched. Unmoved.

Sitting in The White Hart, he had to really push his imagination to try and recall the madness that had clamoured in his head as he'd driven from the burnt emporium to Anna's flat. What had he been thinking?

Rat.

One word. Rat. That had been it. That had been all of it. But for just a moment it had been everything. He'd raced across the city thinking maybe Anna had somehow been involved in the outbreak of violence that had preceded and perhaps even triggered the riots. And so, at her flat, he'd smashed his way in and… nothing.

Nothing at all.

Of course nothing. It didn't make sense.

For a while it had bothered him. Troubled him. He'd worried about her. Still did from time to time. But life had moved on. Things had settled down. The storm had passed and his hope had rallied. As perhaps it always would have. Just the way he was built.

He mulled over these things along with many others as he drank his ale, and when he was done he quietly parked his glass on the table, buttoned up his coat and walked through the pub and out into the garden. He could look east from here, out across the broad stretch of water that reached out towards the sea. He wondered if that stretch of water was a *sound* of water. Don't know. He shrugged and headed down to the gate at the foot of the sloped lawn that opened out onto the footpath that gilded the water's edge all the way back towards home.

The path led south for a few hundred metres before it forked east and south-west. As he took the eastbound fork he saw a young family heading down from the south-west path. Father, mother, young son. He guessed son – young child in a warm hooded coat. Duffel coat. Reminded him of Paddington Bear. The child skipped boyishly on ahead of his parents, looking back every now and then to check they were following, which they were, at a casual amble. The way she held a hand to her belly told Tom that the child skipping down the path towards him would soon have to get his head around not being the sole centre of the universe. They looked happy. He smiled and raised a hand.

They seemed to pause momentarily before the man raised a hand in return.

Tom liked that about this place. That people were so few and far between you could actually greet them in passing. He headed on east and left the family behind him, picking up the pace now as the rapidly increasing gloom of the evening made the shadows ever more impenetrable.

At the outskirts of the village a bunch of kids bundled laughingly past him and cut left down through the gorse bushes to the playing fields and the swings. If they'd been city kids he would have assumed they'd been heading down to the fields to get drunk. Or high. But they're not city kids. They're probably just going to chase each other around and banter. High jinks. Nothing more than that.

He tramped around the last few turns of the gravelled pathway and the cottage swung into view. It couldn't have been more picture-postcard if it tried. That's why he'd chosen it. From the white picket fence to the low ceilings and the rope-swing hanging from the tree in the front garden. Light poured out from every window on the ground floor. He clacked through the gate and up the path to the door. He paused then, and crept round to the kitchen window. He could hear his wife and daughter discussing how much something needed stirring. He peeped in and saw his daughter stood on a chair at the kitchen sideboard, clumsily manhandling a huge wooden spoon and gripping the edge of an enormous bowl. His wife was behind her, ready to pounce the second that spoon, bowl or daughter, or any combination of the above, toppled or took flight across the kitchen. 'OK baby, that's good, let me take it now.'

The young girl, ever the princess, refused to submit control and poked a shoulder out in defiance of her mother's suggestion, tightening her grip on both spoon and bowl, 'Not ready yet Mummy.'

His wife looked up at the ceiling in exasperation, and quietly stamped her own foot.

He almost laughed out loud at that.

Like mother, like daughter.

He tiptoed back to the front door and went through to them.

In the kitchen he walked up behind his wife, slipped his arms round her and nuzzled the back of her neck. 'How my girls doing?'

'Not ready yet Daddy!'

His wife pushed back into his embrace. 'Well this one's about to throttle that one.'

'Yeah?' He put his hands on her tummy and, perhaps inspired by the family he'd seen on the way back from the pub, blurted out before he had a chance to stop, 'Don't want to make another one then?'

She stiffened at that, turned, pushed him back and shot her most deadly serious expression up at him. And she looked so like the little girl fighting with the spoon and the bowl that he couldn't help but burst out laughing. She thumped his chest and melodramatically turned away from him. It didn't help his outburst of giggles any. That little foot-stamp again and he knew now that she was turning it on.

'You're such a bastard.'

He held her again. 'I know. I'm sorry.'

She melted in his arms then. 'You serious?' She whispered.

'I think I might be,' he whispered back.

She took his hands and put them on her belly.

'Maybe…' she said, '…maybe.'

'Not yet Daddy!' the child continued to insist, to the charmed amusement of her parents, '… not yet!'

2

I throw my arm round her waist and pull her to me as we head out into the bitter cold of the early evening. The newborn night. From the garden at the back of the rambling farmhouse we can see along the water to the darkness of the sea. If I were to head down to that water and sail north, eventually I'd hit the ice at the top of the world. No land between here and there. The thought sobers me. Heartens me. It gives everything a sense of scale.

The city is only a few hours distant across the land to our backs, but it might as well be as far away as that ice. That's how distant it is now from our lives. I've not been back since it all was done. Since that life ended and this new one started. I don't miss it. I don't miss anything.

The boy takes my hand and allows me to lead him down through the garden to the path. His hair has grown back darker. It is still fair, but not as fair as in the photographs I have seen in the newspapers. There hasn't been much in the press. Not as much as one might have expected. The occasional melancholic piece by journalists with aspirations to find poetry in the inexplicable urban flare-up that now resides so comfortably in the past for most. The world has faltered on and found new crises to obsess over, greater institutional failings to condemn and deeper existential shortfalls over which to lie awake at night praying for forgiveness. Life moves so fast for them. They always forget. As has the boy now, at last, forgotten.

In those first few weeks after the fire he would not even look at me. His loathing for me was plain. He would not leave Anna's side and he would frequently act out and smash things around the house. It was a hard time for all of us. Not least because the other children had to find their feet too. Space had been tight in the house, but that in turn had given us a focus – something to work towards, something with which to work away from the past.

On the estate there are two large flint-walled outbuildings that had housed decades of junk. The previous owners of the farm had abandoned the accumulated detritus of their lives in these buildings. I hadn't insisted that they clear them when I took on the farm. I saw no reason to. I had been feeling extravagant when I'd bought the place. Extravagant, and flighty – this was between ten and fifteen years ago now, back when the plan to escape him was in its infancy. I couldn't

245

see what I'd need the buildings for and so had shrugged and said no worries.

And so, after everything was done, I had set the flock to work. Clearing the buildings out, and then remodelling them, making them their own.

They'd needed help, of course. Most of them were unskilled – certainly all of the new flock were unskilled – but they were keen to learn. Keen to get busy. Get their hands dirty. It was as if they'd been waiting their whole lives for something to do. The day-crew helped find the right people, with the right skills, who would work through the night with us. That was in fact the biggest challenge. People can be funny about working with the afflicted. Especially those with skin conditions. It's not like there was a sign at the gate, but when the population density is so low whispers have so much more volume. We knew we were 'the leper farm'. It tickled us a little. Better that they dismissed us with that traditional word from the Good Book than know anything closer to the truth. It was convenient. Perhaps more for them (not that they would know it) than for us. But there were plenty out there with minds broad enough to not fear us. To not fear contagion. To want to work with us. Who were happy and decent enough to care.

And besides, we paid well.

So the day-crew expanded to include an architect who worked with the flock to outline the changes needed to the outbuildings. A site manager, and some head labourers to oversee the work. With the flock themselves doing most of the heavy lifting. It took about six months before they could move into the first building. The second was ready three months after that. And then they could spread their wings, and each had their own space.

Of course by the time they'd made space for themselves, the boy had long since settled in. Perhaps the way things had developed between myself and Anna had been a catalyst for that change. At the beginning we both shared our loss of *him*, the old-one. We had both escaped the same oppressive relationship. We both missed him, in a way – in that we both *didn't* miss him – we shared the same ridiculous guilt. We were both elated to be free of him. But terrified that we didn't know how to fly without him. And so we flew together into these new lives. Tentatively. Excitedly.

She took to the boy, and at the beginning was the only one who could calm his rages. Always with love. Her love was the only thing that could cool the fire of his furies. Her patience. Her understanding. It was hard not to love her. And there was no reason I could think of to try and resist. So, I started to love her.

I think for her it happened differently. I think for her I was more complicated. She had more reason for caution. For her, the first small steps towards a relationship were fuelled by a physical hunger. For my male form. Which is funny for us, now, when we talk of it. Of how *unusual* we are. And nothing to do with our 'leprosy'. More to do with the complexities of our gender. My gender. Now. In the sense that for me I grew to love her as a sister. As *her* sister. But to her I was a man. And so she saw me differently. Wanted me differently. And there was plenty of awkwardness. At the start.

But it quickly evaporated beneath the heat of our passion. Our hunger.

And soon enough, we became parents to Peter. And he forgave me. And then he forgot that there was anything to forgive. The flock made their nests, feathered them and bedded in. The farm, and the family, flourished.

Which brings us to now.

Heading down through the garden, my arm round her, Peter holding my hand. Through the gate and out onto the track that leads down towards the fork in the path. As we descend, Peter lets go of my hand, pulls the hood of his coat up against the chill and skips on ahead, humming a song to himself: *Oompa Loompa, do-pi-dee-do!* He has become quite the Dahl fan of late. Which is fitting. I can't help feeling that we have become something that Dahl might once have written a story about. Had the idea occurred to him. Perhaps I'll do it myself. It would be a better tale than the one that brought us here.

I'm lost in these thoughts when Anna freezes. 'Oh my god… it's Tom.'

I look down the path and there, at the fork, heading back from the direction of The White Hart, is a man. He raises his hand and I raise mine in return. I don't think he recognises her. He's too far away. She only recognises him because she is gifted. She hasn't got used to it yet. The man lowers his hand and continues on his way.

'What's he doing here?' Anna asks, her voice gilt-edged with mild panic.

I shrug. 'Probably getting away from the city. Half the

village is owned by folk from the city who rent their places out when they're not here. That's why it's usually half deserted.'

'But what if he *does* see me. What if…'

I swing her round to face me, put my hand on the bump of her belly and smile down into her worried face. 'I doubt he'd recognise you even if he did. You've changed. And even if he did… you'd think of something to say. And I think he'd probably understand. Don't you?'

She considers it, and then weaves her head side to side somewhere between a nod and shaking it. The gesture says *I guess so, maybe.* The baby in her tummy kicks then and both our eyes widen, 'See. Baby says so too.'

She laughs at that and takes my hand and we amble on down to the fork, where we head east, following in the same direction as the man, but comfortably behind him, and moving at a slower pace.

Every evening we take these walks, just before breakfast. The perfect start to our busy nights. There is still some finishing work to be done on the two boarding houses. There are lessons for the kids to be taught – generally reading, writing and numbers. I won't have them being illiterate or innumerate. It simply wouldn't do. I won't have them wasting their time – of which they've now been gifted with such a longer stretch to govern – and I won't stand for them losing sight of themselves, and the world around them: not as *he* did. I need to find a way for us to not punish those that inherit the this earth with hatred. I'm not yet convinced that it's possible. But that is their challenge, *our* challenge. That is the research their current schooling is preparing them for.

Lives of grace and mercy. It won't be easy for them. It won't be easy for any of us.

A small group of the younger ones hurtle past us then, charging down the path towards the swings on the green that nestles in the gorse fields ahead. They chatter and laugh distractedly. 'Careful of people walking!' I call after them.

They'll be careful when they nearly crash into him.

Kids are as kids do. They'll be fine.

John is with them. He still hasn't taken the gift. Other than becoming nocturnal. A contact high. But blood still pumps in his veins. And good for him. He has come along very well. Especially given the loss of his mother. She had been beyond repair and had insisted on skulking back to the city. Back to her old habits. She'd lasted a week. Anna had worried that she might somehow bring us unwanted attention. And so I had threatened the woman as much as was necessary to ensure her silence. It hadn't taken much. She feared us plenty. And I think she wanted nothing more than to forget all about us, whatever it took. Which was fine by me. And fine by John, too, it seemed. But I was glad we'd at least tried. It strengthened John's trust in us, if nothing else. He'd settled, and thrived, ever since. Which made me happy. Makes me happy.

Anna squeezes my hand.

Peter sings.

Oompa Loompa…

A thick, low-slung ground mist greets us at the green. The bigger kids are leaving curlicued jet streams in their wake as they chase each other through it. Peter runs across to join them, and one of them, Megan, drops out from their game to lift him onto a swing. Anna and I sit on the bench silently and watch them. With the mist on the ground and the gorse pluming in black shadows beyond them, they look as if they are running across a cloudscape in the sky. My heart soars, even if it doesn't beat.

I sit there, with my wife, with our child growing in her womb, and our family all about us, hurtling and laughing across the roof of the world, and I know that the past is done, and the future is all to be built. I look at them and bestow the universe to them, because it is not mine to cling on to. It is theirs. It is *theirs*.

Peter swings and swoops and trills, 'Higher! Higher!'

And I second that motion.

Second, third and fourth it. Ad infinitum.

Fly, my pretties! Fly!

For thine is the kingdom.

The power and the glory.

For ever and ever.

Amen.

To those who know, but most especially to Jeanette Adams
for teaching me how, thank you, and madlove, always.